# BAHAMA BREEZE

A NAUTICAL NOVEL

BY
ED ROBINSON

Copyright 2016 by Ed Robinson

This is a work of fiction. Real people and actual places are used fictitiously. Although some of the events described are loosely based on my true life experience, they are mostly products of my imagination.

For the lovely Miss Kim, my true Bahama girl. The blue waters, soft white sand, and sunny skies of the islands, are only enhanced by your beauty.

# Prelude

I realized that I had no mechanism by which to steer my own life. Random events and the whims of others blew me through life's crossroads like a dry leaf in the wind. Maybe this time would be different.

For the lack of any serious goals in my life, I'd long dreamt of spending it on an idyllic island with a beautiful woman. That dream had so far refused to come true. Instead, I was offered a poor man's version of a rich man's dream.

I was going to the Bahamas on someone else's mission. I had a pretty girl aboard. I was getting closer. The pretty girl and I had not yet consummated our relationship, but I was hoping that would soon change.

I was looking for a man. I'd find him. Once my business was concluded, the warm waters of the Bahamas would ease our inhibitions. We'd have too much to drink, and her baggy board shorts would hit the floor at my feet.

That's how I planned it anyway.

# One

He wasn't a fugitive from the law. He was hiding from a man who operated well outside of the law. My ex-lover, Taylor, was in trouble with that man. She owed him a favor. That's where I came in. It was my mission to apprehend the fugitive.

He was holed up in the one and only marina on Great Harbor Cay, in the Berry Islands. I knew a bit about cruising the Bahamas, but I'd never been to Great Harbor. It was off the beaten path. Boats headed south to Nassau or the Exumas never got near it. Boats traveling north to the Abacos passed it by.

His name was Tom Melendez. I was told not to be fooled by the last name. There was nothing Hispanic about him. He was a white-bread honky from Middle America that happened to do tax work and accounting for a crook. His boss had lost a lot of money to a shady financial advisor named Jimi D. He'd taken my money too, but I'd tracked him down and gotten it back. For a fee, I promised to leave Jimi's whereabouts unknown.

Melendez and his boss had a misunderstanding about the financial loss. The tax man decided to take his cut of what was left and disappear. He probably thought he was home free, but his boss was no dummy. A GPS tracker had been planted on the accountant's car, and boat. We knew exactly where he was. All I had to do was make my way into his marina, identify him, and grab him. I'd hold him until his bosses men arrived to take him home. Whatever punishment he received was none of my business. I tried not to think about that.

I had crew for this mission. I picked her up on Grand Cayman. Holly was an American blonde with an island vibe. She'd grown on me over the past weeks. I wanted to think I'd grown on her as well, but I couldn't prove it, at least not sexually. She was twenty years my junior and ambivalent about her sexuality. I held onto my belief that everyone gets horny eventually. If that didn't prove true with Holly, it was still okay. She was nice to be with and I had no surplus of friends.

The job was worth fifty grand. I already had half of it upfront. I'd get the rest from whomever came to pick up my quarry. It would be in cash, of course. Holly knew the deal. I'd tried to send her back to her boat in the Cayman's, but she'd insisted on traveling with me. That was one more reason for me to hold out hope of getting into her pants. Taylor was done with me for good. Nothing was holding me anymore. If things worked out just right, I'd end up in the Bahamas with a pretty girl to share it with. I could just keep on going, island hopping until we found that magic place to settle down together.

Holly and I had spent most of the day doing maintenance chores and making my boat ready for the trip.

"You'd work a little faster without a beer in your hand," she said.

"All work would cease if I had no beer," I countered. "I'd be off in search of beer instead."

"Then get me one before you get too far ahead of me," she said.

I went to get her a beer and thought about how we'd come together. After a shaky start, we'd bonded over intimate conversations. She was easy to talk too. I was a good listener. We shared some secrets and got a good feel for just who each other was. We spent a lot of time alone together, but so far had managed to avoid sex. I'd only approached the subject once. We were both good and sloshed. I was willing. She was not. At least she'd been gracious in her denial of my advances. She let me down in such a way as to make me think it might still be possible some other time. We hadn't gone there again, but I knew the day would come. I'd try again under the right circumstances. She might say yes. If not, I thought we could still remain partners and friends. We'd left her boat down in the Cayman Islands. She'd want it back someday. She had an out if she needed one.

In the meantime, we were off to catch a bad guy, together.

Great Harbor was only about a hundred and fifty miles from Miami, but we were in Punta Gorda, on the opposite coast of Florida. We had a long way to go and we hoped to nab our man before he moved on. We made the boat ready and shoved off early the next day. Holly was a capable captain in her own right. With both of us taking shifts, we could keep steaming instead of stopping to sleep at night. I'd seen the highlights along the way many times. There was no need to explore or take leisure time on this trip. We'd do that in the Bahamas once our work was done.

My trawler, *Leap of Faith,* wasn't fast, but she was sturdy and strong. We cruised at seven knots down Charlotte Harbor, through the Boca Grande Pass and out into the Gulf of Mexico. I set a course south to a point just off Cape Sable, at the bottom of mainland Florida. I figured we'd be rounding the Cape by sunrise. If we made good time, we could watch the sun come up over Florida Bay. I engaged the autopilot and put my feet up on the helm. The day was sunny and calm.

"How are you going to snatch this guy once we find him," asked Holly.

"I don't know," I answered honestly. "I'll size him up first, figure something out."

"So you're just flying by the seat of your pants?" she asked.

"That's how I roll," I answered. "Remember what I taught you?"

"Shit works out," she said. "I know, I know."

We continued motoring south, past Captiva and Sanibel. We stayed inshore along Fort Myers Beach. That's when we ran into the brown water. It came from Lake Okeechobee. It poured into the Caloosahatchee River and made its way into the Gulf at San Carlos Bay. Earlier in the month, Central Florida had seen record rainfall. The Corps of Engineers had to release water from the lake to protect the large earthen dike at its southern border. That water once flowed naturally through the Everglades, before man had better ideas.

Over the past century, the Glades had been drained and claimed for agricultural use. Developers moved in and built houses. Whole towns sprouted up where there used to be swamp. Lake O was overflowing, but the River of Grass was running dry. To complicate matters, crop fields were flooded. The farmers used huge pumps to push that water back into the lake, taking fertilizers and pesticides with it. Now a toxic sludge polluted the once pristine waters we were traveling. It's why I hadn't taken the shorter route across Florida. I couldn't stand to see the damage that was being done. I didn't want to run my boat through the muck either. With the excess fresh water came debris. The lock schedules were all messed up too. I decided it would be easier to go down and around the southern tip of Florida than to cross through that mess.

The brown water continued down to Naples, but began clearing up around Marco Island. We angled away from land at that point, to steer clear of the Cape Romano Shoals.

"How'd did you get into this line of work, Breeze?" asked Holly.

"Just fell into it, I guess," I answered. "Taylor and I were trying to figure things out. She asked me to help an old rich lady up on Lettuce Lake. Some goon doing odd jobs stole some valuables from her. He was living on a boat. I was able to find him and get the goods back. She was a sweet woman. It felt good to be able to help her."

"Did you get paid for that?" she asked.

"She tried to give me thirty grand," I said. "But I didn't need it at the time. She ended up giving it to charity."

"Do you always make that kind of money?" she asked.

"Actually, mostly I do this for myself. I can't seem to keep my hands on my dough. I'm always running someone down to get it back. My stash right now is mostly cocaine money. I hope to hang onto it for a while."

"Other than some good sailing days, my life aboard has been mostly boring," she said. "I had some fool notion that it would be exciting and adventurous. Like your life."

"Trust me," I said. "You could do without the type of excitement I've had. Bullets and bad guys is no way to live. I'd be happy now to just sit on a beach and chill for the rest of my life."

"So why did you take this job?" she asked.

"Excellent question," I replied. "I felt obligated to Taylor for one, but there's more to it than that. Being out here on my boat, with a challenge ahead, that's what fuels my fire. I feel alive when I'm on a mission on some sort. I'm away from the maddening world with no one to bother me, and I ain't bothering no one that don't need bothering."

"So I guess I need a mission for my life," she pondered. "Something to give me some purpose."

"For now, you can have half of this one," I said. "Make yourself useful. Help me with this guy."

"Do I get paid?" she asked.

"One third," I said.

"How's that fair?" she said.

"It's my boat, my expenses," I said. "The boat gets a share. One for me, one for you, and one for the boat."

"Deal," she said. "Now what's one third of fifty grand?"

"Sixteen six, roughly," I said. "Enough to keep you afloat for a while I imagine."

"Hot damn, Breeze," she squealed. "Thanks, man."

It was getting dark and I was getting tired. Holly agreed to take the first night shift. I warned her about the stone crab traps off the Everglades, and the lobster traps in Florida Bay. They'd be hard to see at night. I also warned her not to stray from the course I had set. She'd disobeyed that order down near Cuba and almost gotten us in deep shit. We were in safe waters now, but I knew them better than she did. I didn't want to wake up with the boat aground. I instructed her to wake me after we rounded Cape Sable and entered Florida Bay. I'd made dozens of trips to the Keys, but never took the crossing from the Cape to Islamorada like this time. I'd always gone straight to Marathon or Key West. They called it the Yacht Channel. It was marked but narrow. I wanted to experience it myself rather than let Holly drive us through it.

When you sleep down below with the motor running, the sound can sometimes be bothersome. If the weather is bad or you have something on your mind, it will drive you mad. If all is well, it can actually help lull you to sleep, like running a fan in the room at night just for the noise. That night was a good one. I entertained thoughts of Holly crawling in bed with me to wake me up for a few minutes, then drifted off for a good night's sleep. There were no visions of dead lovers or machine gun fire to haunt me. My mind was clear. My mission was set. All was good.

Holly gave me a nudge and told me to rise and shine. She didn't crawl under the covers. She gave me a quick position report. She said that coffee was made. She retired to her own bunk. I grabbed a mug and climbed up to the bridge to greet the day. The first markers of the Yacht

Channel were in view. The sun was just peeking above the horizon. It was a fine morning. Misty steam rose off the surface of Florida Bay. I could hear droning diesels of lobster boats in the distance. Fishermen in flats boats zoomed across the flats towards their favorite fishing holes. This was the real Florida to me. You couldn't fully appreciate it without a boat. It wasn't Disney World or Miami. It was the Everglades, Florida Bay, and the Gulf of Mexico.

The gauges were all normal. The GPS said we'd join the ICW near Islamorada in a few hours. All I had to do was dodge lobster traps and keep it between the red and green markers. If the weather was forecast to be calm, I planned to go under the Channel Five Bridge and make for Rodriguez Key on the outside of Key Largo. If it was going to blow, I'd stay on the inside and head for Pumpkin Key. We'd wait there for good weather. When the time came we'd exit via Angelfish Creek and make the run to Gun Cay from there. One more day and we'd be at Great Harbor. With two captains aboard, it would be a piece of cake. All we needed was calm seas. I turned the VHF to the weather channel and listened for the pertinent forecast.

The robotic voice informed me that the rest of the day would remain beautiful. Overnight the winds would increase out of the east. The following day would bring winds out of the east/northeast at ten to fifteen. That might not sound bad, but I wanted a day with no northern component to the wind. The Gulf Stream was a powerful current that constantly ran north. Any opposing wind caused the waves to stack up in blocky walls that would pound the shit out of you and your boat. I was in a hurry, but I couldn't risk crossing under those conditions. I headed for Pumpkin Key on the inside. Holly and I would have to find a way to amuse ourselves while we waited for a good window.

I went to wake her at noon, but hesitated. She was curled up like a little girl in her bunk. Her dreads covered half of her face. She wasn't snoring, but her breathes were deep. I watched her breasts rise and fall a few times before turning away. Most women were not at their best while asleep, but she stilled looked pretty. Her natural style and lack of makeup left her looking just as good asleep as when awake. She didn't pack makeup in her things. There was no hair dryer or mirror or other feminine gadgets in her bag. Her entire wardrobe consisted of only shorts, tank tops and bathing suits.

She came up to the bridge as we were leaving Buttonwood Sound and entering Tarpon Basin.

"What are we doing in here?" she asked.

"Winds aren't right," I said.

"It's beautiful," she said. "Let's go out to Rodriguez and jump across in the morning."

"North/northeast tomorrow," I said. "Not good."

"How strong?" she asked.

"Only ten to fifteen," I said. "But anything with north in it is a no-go."

"You're being overly cautious," she said. "Ten to fifteen is child's play."

"How many times have you made this crossing?" I asked.

"I haven't," she said.

"I have," I told her. "Several times. I know what I'm doing. You don't want to be in the Gulf Stream with any north in the wind."

"Okay, if you say so," she said.

She had a little bit of toothpaste in the corner of her mouth. I used my thumb to wipe it off. She let me do it.

"Don't you ever look in a mirror?" I joked.

"I know what I look like," she said.

"You look like an albino Jamaican with that hair," I said. "I think you're pretty, but you'd be a knockout with a nice doo."

"I am what I am, Breeze," she said. "Take it or leave it."

"Calm down now," I said. "Just messing with you. You didn't eat yet did you?"

"No, but I'm hungry," she said.

"Here, take the wheel. I'll make us some lunch while it's calm. Just go right on through Tarpon Basin and into Blackwater Sound. I'll be back in a few."

I went below to round up sandwich fixings. I chuckled because I was paying her sixteen grand, but I was the one preparing lunch. I was pretty sure that was a first. I'd had plenty of women aboard, but none of them could be trusted to navigate without me standing over their shoulder. Holly could handle it.

We shared lunch while taking in the scenery. The water was clear but dark in Blackwater Sound. It turned blue again as we entered Card Sound. Pumpkin Key was just off Snapper Point, at the northernmost part of Key Largo.

We anchored off the southwest corner to shield ourselves from whatever winds would build overnight.

"What do you want to do now?" Holly asked.

"Let's go catch dinner," I said. "You like to fish don't you?"

"I like to fish, but would you rather have lobster?" she asked.

"Hell yeah," I said. "Sounds awesome."

"I saw a rock pile coming in here," she said. "I bet there's some bugs on it."

I launched the dinghy while Holly changed into a bikini. She didn't move like a girl in a bikini normally does. She was agile, but not particularly graceful. She was athletic, but in a gangly, loose way. Her body screamed femininity. Her motions did not. She was just one of the guys, with the tits and ass of a woman.

She directed me to the rock pile. As soon as we got close she slid overboard and dove to the bottom. She swam like a dolphin. She held her breath for several minutes while she poked and prodded in the rocks. She surfaced with one hand high, holding a legal sized lobster. She hung onto the side of the dinghy while I stuffed it in a canvas bag. She caught her breath for a few minutes. I just looked at her all dripping wet, a big smile on her face.

"Just earning my keep," she said, diving below the surface again.

Within a minute she had another one. I stowed it with the first one as she struggled to climb aboard. Seeing her difficulty, I tried to give her a hand. She flung a leg over the side in a most unladylike manner and flopped over onto me. We ended up in something that resembled an embrace. Our faces were very close together. She gave me a look as if to say *Oh great, he's going to kiss me now.*

"May I?" I asked.

"How polite of you to ask first," she said. Then she nodded.

We put our lips together for a split second, then retreated. She turned her eyes away. I took her chin in my hand and turned her back to me. We tried again, longer this time. It was salty and sweet. Then it was over.

"Come on," she said. "Let's go steam these babies up."

It was progress.

# Two

We awoke the next morning to winds out of the northeast at fifteen knots. It was a fine day, but not a good one for crossing the Gulf Stream. I'd made the right call. We were discussing it over breakfast when I remembered that Holly had a phone.

"What kind of weather resources do you have on that thing?" I asked.

"Whatever you want," she replied. "National Weather Service, Weather Underground."

"See what's predicted for tomorrow and the next day," I said. "Look at the offshore forecast between here and Gun Cay first. Then look at the Great Bahama Bank for day two."

She fiddled with the device for ten minutes,

checking multiple sources. She concluded that it was good news. The next day's forecast called for light winds out of the southeast. The following day looked to be devoid of wind on the Banks. We had a near perfect two-day window to get to Great Harbor. We just had to wait until morning.

I climbed up to the bridge to work with the chart plotter. I laid in a dead reckoning course from the mouth of Angelfish Creek to the Gun Cay Cut. I tried to remember the calculations for set and drift. The direction of the current is called the set. The speed of that current is called drift. I ignored wind speed and direction as they probably wouldn't be much of a factor. The Gulf Stream constantly pushes north at varying speeds between two and four miles per hour. I had to get out the paper charts, in this case the Explorer Guides, to draw actual lines with a pencil. I hadn't done this type of figuring in a long time. Eventually, I settled on a course that would take us almost exactly due east as we entered the Stream. The current would push us northward. The rate of push was only an estimate. I'd have to make small changes along the way.

Holly came up and I went through it all over

again to show her how I did it. Instead of a straight line to Gun Cay, we'd leave a curved trail, adding some miles to the trip. I estimated it to be sixty miles. At seven knots we'd make it in less than nine hours. The Stream would increase our speed for part of the way, so eight and a half looked reasonable. We could leave at first light and have plenty of daylight left when we got to Gun Cay.

During the wait, an awkward feeling hung in the air, left over from the previous day's kiss. Neither of us mentioned it. We spent some time stowing or securing everything that might move around during our crossing. Then we went fishing.

The mangrove points on either side of the entrance to Angelfish creek looked like a good place to start. The current rolled around the corners close to shore. The roots and branches hung out over deeper water. It was a perfect spot for a redfish or a snook to lie in ambush. I drove the dinghy up inside the creek a bit, killed the motor, and let it drift back out towards the bay. Holly casted to the north shore. I tossed my lure at the south side. We hooked up almost simultaneously. I'd tricked a husky red out of his hiding spot. Holly did battle with a sleek snook. We each landed our catch with assorted hoots and hollers.

"Which one should we keep for dinner?" I asked.

"Hell, keep them both," she said. "We'll have half of each tonight, save the rest for tomorrow."

"Sounds good," I said.

We continue to catch and release for another hour. Eventually we fished out the banks of the river mouth. We went back to the boat, leaving sore lips and hurt feelings all along the mangroves.

Holly ate with gusto. She had a strong appetite. She caught me staring at her while she shoveled blackened redfish into her mouth. She stopped eating and stared back. Her eyes were a soft blue. I'd never really noticed them before. Her nice breasts and dread-locked hair always drew my attention away from her eyes.

"Quit being a goofball and eat your fish," she said.

"How do you stay so thin with that appetite?" I asked.

"It's fish," she said. "I like to fish. I like to eat fish, and rice. I never have money to eat much else."

"Don't go getting all fat after we get paid, then," I joked. "You'll have money for burgers and steak."

"Ice cream," she said. "I'd really love some ice cream."

I didn't have any ice cream on the boat. I never did. It didn't mix well with beer and it took up too much space in the freezer. I told her we'd certainly find some in the Bahamas. I offered her rum instead, but she declined. She wanted to have a clear head in the morning.

"You nervous about the crossing?" I asked.

"Not really," she answered. "Just excited. Looking forward to it."

"Me too," I admitted. "I'm glad you came along."

"Same here," she said. "Good night, Breeze."

She went to her bunk and left me with the dirty dishes. As I cleaned up our mess, I felt the air for sexual tension. I couldn't detect a hint. I thought back to previous women on previous trips. Andi was so hot and sensual that I'd lived in a constant state of arousal. When she finally offered herself to me, I was quick to take advantage. Yolanda was innocent and sweet. I'd fantasized about making love to her, but when she came to me one night I turned her away. Sex with Joy had just been playtime. We never took it seriously.

Holly hadn't made up her mind if she wanted a physical relationship with me or not. I was an old guy in her eyes. She belonged on a beach playing volleyball with a bunch of thirtysomethings. Something was there, though. She liked me. She'd confided in me a little bit. I suspected there was a lot more to know. Whatever damage she'd suffered in this cruel life caused her to stay reserved. Meanwhile, the air lacked any sign of sexual energy. Whatever key that might unlock her desires was unknown to me.

The sun had not yet risen when she yanked my covers off and rousted me out of bed.

"Come on, Captain," she said cheerfully. "We've got an ocean to cross."

"What's the wind doing?" I asked.

"There's hardly any wind at all," she said. "Fire this mother up. Let's go."

"Coffee," I said. "Coffee first."

"It's brewing," she said. "Let's get this show on the road."

She was all smiles and full of cheer. Good for her. I got a cup of coffee and joined her on the back deck. After a few sips, her good mood rubbed off on me. The sun was about to come up. The water was flat. Just a hint of moving air could be detected.

"It's going to be a good day," I said. "Shake the bridle off the anchor chain. I'll start her up."

"Hot damn," she yelped. "We're going to the Bahamas."

She continued to smile and laugh all day. Her mood was infectious. The Gulf Stream was nothing but a mill pond that day. It may have been the most enjoyable journey I'd ever taken. The boat ran like a finely tuned machine. The deep blue water reflected a brilliant sun. The air was clean and crisp. The strong current in the center of the stream increased our speed to almost nine knots. It was glorious.

"What do have that we can troll with?" asked Holly.

"That big spinning rod has fifty pound test braid on it," I said. "There's a brand new Mahi killer on top of the box."

"I'll rig it up," she said. "Let's get us a Mahi."

She was faster at tying knots than I was. She readied the rig and deployed it in a few minutes. She stayed at the rod holder, letting out line. Once she was happy with how it was running, she rejoined me at the helm.

"This is awesome, Breeze," she said. "I can't wait to poke around in the islands. I bet the snorkeling is fantastic. Do you dive much?"

"Not unless I have to," I said. "Why jump off a perfectly good boat?"

"To see what you can see," she said. "Fish, coral, all sorts of critters."

"I can hold my breath for about five seconds," I said. "And my ears start popping below six feet."

"We'll have to work on that," she said. "I'll help you."

"I'm more interested in that skinny dipping we talked about," I joked.

"Breeze junior flapping in the wind?" she laughed.

"And Holly's bare ass baking in the sun," I replied.

"We're going to have such a good time," she said.

The rod went down. Line started screaming off the reel. We both lunged for it. Holly elbowed me out of the way and got there first. We'd hooked something huge. She tightened the drag one click. Line continued disappearing at a rapid rate.

"If you tighten it too much, it will break," I said.

"We're going to lose all the line," she said.

"Hold on," I yelled. "I'll try backing down on it."

*Leap of Faith* was no fishing boat. She was not nimble. She didn't back up for shit. I tried it anyway. Holly was screaming that we were almost out of line. I gunned it in reverse. Water sloshed over the transom. The fish ran off to our starboard. I swung the boat around and drew even with it. Holly was getting back some line. That's when it happened.

A Blue Marlin broke the surface, walked on its tail, and shook its head violently back and forth. The water it threw off made little rainbows in its wake. It hung suspended for a split second. Then it was gone. Our tackle was no match for it. Still, it was an amazing sight to see. I'd never been much for offshore fishing, but I had a new appreciation for it. Holly was whooping and screaming like she'd landed the damn thing.

"Did you see that son-of-a-bitch?" she yelled. "That was incredible."

"I saw it, girl," I yelled back. "It was beautiful."

"We need bigger tackle," she said. "Make a waypoint. We'll catch that bastard on the way back."

I marked the spot on the GPS and named it Marlin. Holly was digging through the box for another lure. She wasn't happy with my meager selection. She finally settled on a Crystal Minnow with stout hooks. We trolled it for several more hours without a bump.

Our speed slowed as we left the Stream. We'd made great time. We approached the lighthouse just to the north of the cut and hugged the shoreline of Gun Cay. Just to be cautious, I slowed way down, but the water stayed deep and no rocks reached up to grab us. It was early enough in the day that I still had the sun over my shoulder. Visibility was excellent. I swung north after we cleared the cut and looked for a likely place to anchor. Holly went to the bow to look for a clear, sandy spot. On her signal, I dropped the hook and backed down on it. We held on the first try. I let the engine idle down for a few minutes, before shutting everything down.

"That's it," I said. "We're here."

"Nothing much to see but that lighthouse," she said. "Still, it's pretty cool to be here. How long is tomorrow's leg?"

"All day and then some," I said. "If you're game for leaving in the dark, we might make it by nightfall."

"I ain't scared," she said. "We'll turn in early."

"But first we make a toast," I said.

I poured two glasses of rum, no ice.

"To Holly's first marlin, and first Gulf Stream crossing," I said, raising my glass to hers.

"To Captain Breeze," she said, clinking her glass to mine.

She put her glass down and reached out both hands to me. I took her hands. She stepped in close, looking me in the eyes. We kissed. Slowly and gently we found a fit for our mouths. We lingered. She hugged me ever so lightly. When we parted she looked down at the deck.

"I don't know what's going to happen on this trip, Breeze," she said. "But thank you for this. I can feel myself coming alive."

"The pleasure is all mine," I said. "I don't know what's going to happen either, but I can tell you one thing."

"Shit works out," she said.

"That's right, young grasshopper," I said. "One way or another it will work out. I'll try not to sweat it if you don't."

"Deal," she said.

We bumped fists to seal the agreement. With anyone else I would have felt foolish bumping fists. With her, it seemed appropriate. Maybe I was coming alive too.

# Three

The trip across the Banks had an eerie quality to it. The depths held steady at eight to ten feet. The water was so clear we could make out every detail of the bottom. The seas were glass. The few coral heads we encountered were deep, but it was hard to determine just how deep in the clear water. The boat seemed to float on air as we glided eastward.

I had tried my best to get Holly liquored up the previous night, but it didn't work. She really didn't drink that much. I needed to reevaluate that part of my plan. Our kiss had been pleasant, but not passionate. She was moving very slowly, if she was moving in my direction at all. I saw real passion in her when she hooked that marlin. She wasn't shy when we fished off the dinghy or she dove for lobsters, but whenever we drew physically close, she held back. I'd promised not to sweat it, so I dropped that train of thought.

There was no wind, but there must have been a slight current. We were traveling at just below seven knots. We wouldn't make the marina at Great Harbor much before dark. I decided I didn't care. I was enjoying Holly's company so much. We could just anchor out again. We'd spend another day alone together before rejoining society. Once we were in the marina, our attentions would turn to capturing the man we came for.

When I stopped short of the marina entrance and prepared to drop anchor in Bullock's Harbor, Holly wanted to know why we didn't go on in.

"Customs doesn't work past four or five o'clock," I said. "We don't want to make some poor joker work overtime. It's not a good way to make nice with them."

"You know a lot about this stuff," she said.

"I've never been this far north in the Bahamas," I said. "But I've been all through the southern chain. The Exumas, the out islands, down to the Turks and Caicos. I've been to the DR a couple times. Puerto Rico, USVI and the BVI."

"Holly crap," she said. "You and this old boat have been around."

"You can add the Chesapeake, Galveston, and of course Grand Cayman to the list," I said proudly.

"That's a lot of adventure," she said. "I value your experience. I want to do all that. I want to go to South America, through the Panama Canal, and on to Fiji."

"This boat could never make it," I said. "You're on your own there."

"My boat can do it," she said. "But I can't do it by myself."

"Is that an invitation?" I asked.

"It's just a dream," she answered. "I've got a lot to learn first. Maybe someday."

I tried to think of something profound to say about "maybe someday", but nothing clever came to mind. It was time to quit being distracted by her and get down to the business at hand. Once in a slip at the marina, we'd observe this Tom Melendez. After sizing him up, I'd figure out a way to proceed.

"You afraid of a confrontation with this guy?" I asked.

"I have no idea what to expect," she said. "Should I be worried?"

"I don't know," I admitted. "The plan is to use as little violence as possible, but keep on your toes."

"Tell me about some of the other times," she said. "You just don't seem like a violent guy to me."

"My first real brush with trouble caused me to smack a guy in the head with a hammer," I said. "I let him live. He came back and shot a bunch of holes in the boat. I don't know how I didn't piss my pants."

"Let's avoid that sort of thing this time," she said.

"My second big mission was to track down and confront a ninety pound woman," I said. "She tried to rip my throat out with her teeth, but it worked out in the end."

"What did you do?" she asked.

"I screwed her brains out," I said. "Calmed her right down."

"Sounds like something out of a James Bond movie," she said.

"I was dumb with that guy in Texas," I said. "I underestimated him. I thought I'd just walk in and kick his ass. It didn't work out that way."

"He kick your ass instead?" she asked.

"Pretty much," I admitted. "But I managed to take him down. Shit worked out."

"I sit here and look at you," she said. "I'm getting to know you. It's just hard to envision all these heroics. It's hard to see you as a dangerous man."

"Taylor thought she wanted a dangerous man," I said. "But when shit got real she changed her mind."

"Her loss," she said.

"Most recently, I bonked a mobster in the head with a cue ball," I continued. "When he didn't go down, I smacked him with a pipe. He was still standing, so I took out a knee."

"Jesus, Breeze," she said. "There's a lot more to you than I knew."

"I didn't ask for any of it," I told her. "Life comes at you and you deal with it as best you can."

"That kind of stuff doesn't happen to someone in the real world," she said. "Normal people don't even know that kind of stuff happens at all."

"That's true, I guess," I said. "I'm still looking for that quiet little cove to waste away my days in peace, but first, we've got a mission to complete."

"You get off on it, don't you?" she asked. "These sticky situations give you a thrill."

"I could really do without the stickiness," I said. "But I suppose I like having a mission."

"That's what I've been lacking," she said. "I've just been aimless."

"Right now our aim is to apprehend one Tom Melendez," I said. "After that, we'll think of something else to get into."

"I could do the quiet coves and beaches for a little while," she said. "I've really got no place else to be."

"That's wonderful, Holly," I said. "Looking forward to it."

I called the marina in the morning to get a slip assignment. The dock master, Hans, was as pleasant as he could be. I had Holly to help with lines, but I requested someone at the dock as well, just to be safe. As we approached the slip, I saw three men on the pier. Two wore marina uniform shirts. The third man was wearing swim trunks and a tank top. He had a beer in his hand. We tossed the lines and together we all put *Miss Leap* smoothly in her slip. I handed the dock hand a ten. Hans refused to take my money. I asked for Customs and Immigration and the dock master promised to summons them.

"My name's Tom," the third man said. "Welcome neighbor."

Tom Melendez was a stocky fellow. He was an inch shorter than I was, but he was twice as thick. He had broad shoulders, a big chest and big upper arms. His spiked blond hair made him appear younger than he probably was. I guessed mid to late forties. He didn't look like an accountant. I hoped that his time behind a desk had made him soft. He looked like he could have played football in his younger days. I wasn't too sure about getting into a tussle with him. He just smiled as I sized him up.

"Let me get you a beer, man," he said.

"Breeze," I said. "The name's Breeze."

"Hey, cool name, buddy," he said, as he boarded his own boat.

It was a newer model Silverton Sedan. It looked to be thirty-six foot in length. It was in good shape. I walked behind the transom, checking it out. The boat's name was *Bat Cave*. It wasn't a serious cruising boat, nor a fishing vessel. It was the kind of boat that someone would buy, if they didn't know much about boats. It was good for entertaining, or casual sunset cruises. It wouldn't be much of a voyager. Tom popped back out with two more beers.

"That's a sweet old trawler," he said. "Where did you come in from?"

"We came across from Key Largo," I told him.

I didn't want to mention Punta Gorda. If he was smart, he might make the connection.

"You'll like it here," he said. "Plan on staying a while? Most of these other folks are old geezers. The parties end real early."

"Not sure yet," I said. "Well check it out. Maybe stay a week."

"Enjoy your time," he said. "I'll see you around."

He walked back up the dock. He had a handshake or a high-five for everyone he encountered along the way. He never quit smiling. He was having the time of his life. I was about to change that. I kind of felt bad for him. Holly had been securing extra lines and plugging in water and electric. My little chat with Tom had gotten me out of the chores.

"What do you think?" she asked. "Tough guy or sissy?"

"He's big enough," I said. "Our advantage is that he doesn't have a clue. He thinks he's safe here."

"How do you want to play it?" she asked.

"Looks like he'd be easy to get good and drunk," I answered. "Let's have a party. Wait till he passes out and tie him up."

"I can feed him rum till he drops," she said.

"Good idea," I said. "Be real friendly and keep pouring. He won't be able to resist you."

I think she blushed a little bit. Whenever I complimented her looks, she did that. Her self-esteem needed a boost, or she was nervous about me finding her attractive. I wasn't sure which one.

We finished securing the boat and checking on systems. All was fine. Customs came and checked us in. They were professional and pleasant. We each got new stamps for our passports. It felt good to know that I was legal again. I'd snuck through the Bahamas without showing my papers to anyone a time or two. I'd cleared all that up though. I was now legit. We raised the Bahamian courtesy flag and checked in with Hans at the marina office.

The facilities, though not new, were very clean and orderly. The staff were friendly and professional. The fixed docks were in good repair. I liked it. It wasn't the fanciest place I'd ever stayed, but it was homey. Hans obviously ran a tight ship. He showed us the showers and the laundry and explained rates and water usage. They had two water supplies. One was untreated well water not fit for drinking. It was free. The other was treated by reverse osmosis and good to drink. It was fifty cents per gallon. They had a small grocery store on premises, as well as a restaurant with a pool. There was a somewhat larger store just up the road.

"How long will you be staying with us, Mr. Breeze?" Hans asked.

"Just Breeze is fine," I said. "Not sure. Maybe only a few days. We needed to check in to the country and we heard this was a good place to do it."

"Welcome to our island, and our marina," he said. "I can take your credit card information and we can settle up upon departure, if you wish."

"Is cash okay?" I asked.

"Cash will do just fine, sir," he answered. "Enjoy your visit. There will be a potluck dinner at the tiki tonight at six, if you are so inclined."

"Sure, that will be great."

We had all day to kill, so I suggested walking to the other side of the island. I'd heard about an awesome beach and I wanted to check it out. The walked turned out to be a long one, but it was worth it. A long stretch of white powdery sand stretched out in both directions. The shallow, blue water was crystal clear. We both just stood there in awe for a moment.

"This is what I dreamed the Bahamas to be," Holly said.

"Lots of awesome beaches all over the Bahamas," I told her. "This is a real good one though."

"There's no people," she said.

"Just us," I said. "Let's walk."

We walked the beach for hours, stopping to poke at shells and debris from time to time. We sat on a downed log to rest. The sun was high and the heat was on. After ten minutes, Holly gave me a mischievous grin. She stood up, took off her shirt, and dropped her shorts. She sprinted down into surf and out into the water, diving and staying under for a long time. She finally popped up about a hundred yards offshore.

"Come on, chicken" she yelled. "The water's fine."

It was no time to be modest. I quickly got naked and sprinted after her. I had to come up for air fifty yards short. She was laughing and splashing like a kid in a pool. Water beaded up on her dreads and gave them a sparkly look.

"You surprised me," I said.

"I think I surprised myself," she said. "The water, the beach, it's all so beautiful. I just couldn't help myself."

"You only add to the beauty of the scene," I said. "Really, Holly, your body is pretty hot under those baggy shorts."

"I have a hard time seeing it that way," she said. "I've always been a dork. I don't fit in anywhere."

"You fit in just fine here," I said. "Dork is not a word I could ever use to describe you."

"You don't fit in either," she said. "Or we wouldn't be here in the first place."

"So I'm a dork too?" I asked.

"You're a dork fish," she laughed.

She splashed me and turned to swim away. I watched her strong smooth strokes as she put distance between us. She was the fish, I thought to myself. I could barely swim. She turned towards shore and eventually stood up. We started walking towards each other, chest deep in the water. She stayed just deep enough to keep her breasts covered. When we met, I took her hand and led her back towards the beach, and our clothes. We walked together naked when the water got shallow enough to expose our bodies.

"This is weird," she said.

"You started it," I answered.

"Maybe I should have waited until dark," she said.

"It's okay," I told her. "I feel weird too. Let's get dressed."

# Four

When we got back to the marina, we saw a few folks already setting up for the potluck dinner Hans had told us about. We went back to the boat to change. I put on my best shirt. It made me think of Andi. She bought it for me, but I couldn't remember where. Time has a way of healing wounds and erasing memories. I wondered where she was now, how she was doing. Holly came out in a slightly wrinkled sun dress.

"Is this going to be okay?" she asked.

"It's perfect," I said. "These people are boaters. They understand a few wrinkles."

"I get self-conscious at social events," she said. "Don't leave me along with strangers."

"We don't have to stay long," I said. "I just want to talk to Tom. We'll invite him over for dinner or something."

Tom was at the tiki when we arrived. He had compliments for all the ladies. *Your dress is so pretty, Angie. Your hair looks nice, Jane.* He complimented the men too. *That's a real cool boat you got there, Bob. Looking fit Jim, you been working out?* He was the life of the party. He moved from couple to couple, keeping old conversations going and starting new ones. He carried an iPod that played island tunes. I recognized some Trop Rock with some raggae mixed in.

"Hey, Breeze, old buddy," said Tom. "You and the misses having a good time?"

"It's nice here," I said. "Thanks for the kind welcome."

"I wish you'd stick around," he said. "Bring some youth and excitement to this bunch."

"Come on over for dinner tomorrow night," I said. "We'll drink ourselves silly and swap lies all night long."

"Just what the doctor ordered," said Tom. "You're on. Can I bring something?"

"Just some beer," I said. "Holly will catch us some fish. I've got plenty of rum onboard."

"Aarrggh," said Tom. "All good pirates like to drink the demon rum. I'll be there."

We snuck out soon after that. I don't think Holly said ten words at the dinner gathering. She pulled off her dress as soon as we got inside the salon. She was wearing a bikini top as a bra. She had a tank top and board shorts in seconds. She let out a deep sigh and plopped down on the settee.

"That was more awkward than walking naked on the beach," she laughed. "I hate those things."

"Tomorrow night we nab Tom," I said. "Then we can vacate the premises. Find some more deserted beaches."

"How do you want to work it?" she asked.

"We keep him out there on the back deck," I began. "Make him comfortable. After a few beers we start doing rum shots. His glass is rum. Our glasses will be water. Laugh at his jokes and keep the shots coming. Flatter him."

"What if he doesn't pass out?" she asked.

"He'll be drunk enough that I can bring him down," I said.

"Then what?"

"Then we use zip ties. Bind his hands and feet together," I said. "He won't be able to hop around and club us with both arms."

"He's going freak when he wakes up," she said.

"I guess we'll gag him too then," I said.

"How long until they come pick him up?" she asked.

"Give me your phone," I said. "I'll call and tell them we'll have him the next morning early. They can get a head start."

Tom showed up with a twelve pack of beer. He'd stuffed the cardboard case full of ice to form a makeshift cooler. I gave him my chair. He propped his feet up on the transom just like I normally did.

"This is the life, ain't it Breeze?" he said.

"Make yourself comfortable," I said. "Holly is cooking up some snappers she pulled out of the mangroves."

I went inside to check on dinner. I'd found out earlier that Holly wasn't much of a gourmet. She mostly grilled or fried her fish. I had mixed up some white wine and butter and sautéed them instead. We diced a mango into the rice and poured some of the wine sauce over that too. It looked delicious. I took Tom a plate and dug another beer out of his box for him. He was completely at ease. He had no idea what was about to take place. He was happy. He constantly wore a great big smile. He laughed a lot. Holly started pouring rum shots soon after we finished eating.

Tom told us how he botched his docking at Bimini. He wasn't real experienced with his boat. The current got him and he bounced off several pilings before finally tying off. The next day, he figured out how far it was across the Banks. He'd run his Silverton hard and burned a bunch of fuel in the process. He'd had no idea that it would burn forty gallons per hour at full throttle. He laughed at his own ignorance. Apparently, money wasn't an issue.

He was handling the rum pretty well. I was worried he'd really drink all night, but around eleven, he started to slur his speech. His eyes got heavy too. Holly brought shots even more frequently. We didn't even pretend to drink ours anymore. By midnight we couldn't understand what he was saying at all. He continued to tell his stories though. I went inside to use the head. When I came out, he was asleep in the chair, chin resting on his chest. I stood over him for a minute, listening to him breath. He was out.

I motioned for Holly to bring me the zip ties. I looked up and down the docks to verify that no one was looking. All the senior citizens had gone to bed hours before. I should have been sleepy myself, but adrenaline had me wide awake. Holly's eye looked wide too. I put his wrists together and bound them. Holly did the same to his ankles. We didn't have a gag. I decided to drag him inside and close the door behind us. He was damn heavy. Holly gave me a hand and we managed to get him through the door. After plopping him down I looked for something to put over his mouth. An old bandana did the trick.

We stood back and surveyed our work. Tom wasn't going anywhere. We did a silent fist bump and I whispered for her to give me her phone. I made the call. The men who wanted Tom were in Freeport. A boat was bringing them over in the morning. They were to arrive at noon.

"Now we wait," I told Holly. "I think I'll get some sleep."

"I can't sleep with him lying there like that," she said. "I'll watch him."

"Good," I said. "Wake me if something happens."

I got to sleep for three hours. I heard Tom banging about. I jumped up and bumped into Holly in the hallway. She was coming to wake me. We returned to the salon to find Tom on the floor. He was mumbling through his gag. His eyes were filled with terror. I told him if he'd keep his voice to a whisper, I'd remove the bandana. He nodded. I saw tears in his eyes.

"What are you doing, man?" he asked.

"I got paid a lot of money to package you up," I told him. "Your boss would like you returned to him. Some guys are on the way to pick you up."

"Why?" he asked. "You seem like a nice guy. Why would you do this?"

"I do odd jobs now and then," I said. "It's nothing personal."

"You don't understand," he said. "They're not going to take me back. They're going to put a bullet in my head. I'm a dead man. Sure as shit."

"I'm just doing my job," I said. "I can't worry about the rest of it."

"Dude, that's cold," he said. "You can't do this. You gotta let me go."

"Breeze, he's right," said Holly. "We can't do this. I don't want any parts of a man dying because of us. That's not what I signed up for."

I helped him back up to a sitting position. I gave him the opportunity to speak his piece.

"It's that hot bitch lawyer's fault," he began. "The boss dealt with her all the time. He trusted her. She was the one who told me about Jimi D. Some associates used him too. It all seemed on the up and up. The money was supposed to be in the Cayman Islands, safe and hidden from the IRS. I didn't steal it. Jimi D. stole it. He's the one they ought to be trying to find."

Holly gave me a look from hell. She knew. She knew I'd found Jimi D. Now this man's life was at stake. I'd gotten her involved and she was not happy about it. It was one those moments when you just want to hang your head and ask how things could get so fucked up.

"Untie him, Breeze," said Holly. "Help him get out of here."

I had no choice but to obey. If I let them take him, Holly would be gone forever. Besides, I really didn't want his death on my conscience. Taylor hadn't said anything about killing him. It was all supposed to be so simple.

"Cut him loose now, Breeze," Holly demanded. "We've got to get out of here too."

She was right. We couldn't stay here. There would be hell to pay if they showed up and we didn't deliver what they came for. This was spinning out of control quickly. I cut Tom loose and helped him stand.

"Get on that boat and get out of here," I told him.

"The tracker," said Holly. "There's a GPS tracker on your boat."

"Shit, I forgot," I said. "Look, all three of us right now. Get flashlights. We find the damn thing first. Let's move."

Tom said that he always locked his boat, so it had to be outside the cabin somewhere. He started opening lockers and compartments. Holly went up to the bridge to search. We didn't know what it looked like or how it operated. The clock was ticking though. We searched on. It was Holly who finally found it.

The boat had a stainless arch that supported various antennas. She climbed it like a monkey and saw the device attached to the hardtop. It had a clear view of the sky and it couldn't be seen except from above. I stuck it on top of the dock box. To anyone looking, it would appear that Tom's boat was still in the slip. We didn't have much time to put distance between us and them. We had to move fast.

"You're clear to start that thing up and go," I told Tom. "You got fuel?"

"I don't know where I'm going," he said. "I don't know nothing about this cruising stuff."

"You have charts?" I asked. "Do you know how to use them?"

"There was a trail on the GPS leftover from the previous owner," said Tom. "That's how I got here. It only goes back to Miami."

"Let him follow us," Holly said. "We got him into this mess."

I hated the idea, but I went along with it. There was no time to come up with an alternate plan. I'd teach him how to navigate later. Hell, I didn't know where we were going next. I asked Holly to bring me the guide books while I started the engine. Tom fired up his boat. All the lines were untied and together we snuck out of the marina. I found the Berry Islands in the chart book and studied it for a few minutes. We were on the west side of Great Harbor Cay. It looked like the majority of boat traffic would be on the west. Freeport was to the west. A cruise ship dock was to the north at Little Stirrup Cay. In order to go south, we'd have to travel far to the west to avoid shoals. It was a long run to the next port at Chub Cay.

I looked at the western side of the Berry's chain. The chart showed a shallow water, inside route that could be accessed at Market Fish Cay. There was a host of isolated anchorages with good protection along that route. I made up my mind. We turned north and rounded the top of the chain, passing the cruise ship stop before sunup. Tom followed us closely. It was rough out on the Atlantic side and we got tossed around on the way south. Dishes that we hadn't put away clattered below us. *Leap of Faith* was on the run again. It was a situation she was all too familiar with.

I found Market Fish Cay and ducked behind the island. The water calmed. Holly and I were both beat. She hadn't slept a wink. I looked for the first reasonable spot to anchor. I dropped the hook in twelve feet of water, close to a beach on the backside of Market Fish Cay. Tom followed suit, although he had trouble doing it. I don't think he'd ever anchored before. I couldn't babysit him right then. I'd gotten him away. We all needed rest. We could regroup later.

# Five

I couldn't sleep. My mind was a stew of negative thoughts about Taylor and Jimi. Taylor had set me up as an accessory to murder. She hadn't flinched when she offered me fifty grand to track down Tom Melendez. She had to know what was going to happen to him after I collared him. It was hard for me to imagine that she was really that cold inside. Maybe it was her life or his? I couldn't know how much trouble she was in for suggesting Jimi D. as an investment counselor.

The blame was really Jimi's, after all. His theft had jeopardized people's lives. Certainly Tom's life was at risk, maybe Taylor's too. What about

Breeze? I had taken twenty-five grand as a down payment on the job. I didn't complete that job to the payer's satisfaction. They wouldn't be happy about it, but would they come after me? I doubted it. I was in no mood for running from a shadow again.

I couldn't absolve myself of some of the blame either. I'd jumped at the chance to take on another mission. My relationship with Taylor had blinded me to the potential dangers. She was turning about to be a big bag of bad news. I wanted to call her and bitch her out, tell her what a mess she was. I'd had the hints of her immoral side. I just ignored them. I was okay with it when she was on my side. She'd used my money to bribe a judge. I'd avoided a jail term thanks to her knowledge of the seedy side of Florida's judicial system. I was grateful for it then. I couldn't have predicted it would lead to this.

It had taken Holly's stern rebuke to open my mind to what was going down. She wasn't talking to me now. If we were near civilization, she'd probably walk away from the mess I'd gotten her into. I could only hope that we would reconcile once we got rid of Tom.

I was now responsible for Tom. I didn't want to be responsible for him. He needed to gather his resources and help himself. We were going to have to leave this place. We needed to stay on the move until we could determine if we were being hunted or not. We had Holly's phone, complete with a Bahamian SIM card, but we needed to get closer to a tower to make calls. I got up and opened a bottle of rum. Holly was asleep. I took one long pull off the bottle and laid back down. It was just enough to settle my mind. I put Taylor, Tom and Jimi D. out of my thoughts and got some rest.

When I woke up, Holly wanted to know what the plan was. She said that Tom had waved and shrugged from his back deck. He wanted to know what the plan was too. The only thing I knew to do was fall back on my old standby plan, run.

"Let's put some more distance between us and the marina," I told Holly. "We'll head south and look for a cell tower. I need to make some calls."

I waved to Tom and pointed at my bow. I walked up to it and pretended to pull up the anchor chain. He saw what I was doing and understood. I heard his engines start up.

I fired up *Leap of Faith* and Holly prepared to raise the anchor. I idled over close enough to Tom's boat to hold a quick conversation. I asked about his fuel level. He said he had half-full tanks. I told him to follow me. Stay off the radio. We'd anchor again when we picked up a cell signal. He understood.

To save time I went back outside into the Atlantic. We motored past Hoffman Cay, Little Harbor, Bonds and Whale Cay. We started picking up a few bars on Holly's phone. We tucked in behind Frazer's Hog Cay, just off the Berry Island's Club. Tom struggled getting his hook set once again. I tried to figure out how to use Holly's phone to get us out of the mess we were in. Who to call?

I decided on Jimi D. He'd given me his card on my last day in Grand Cayman. He'd offered me a job of sorts. It was funny, thinking back on it. He'd stolen my money. I tracked him down ready to do him great bodily harm. Instead, he'd given it all back and we got drunk together. He paid me an extra hundred grand to keep his whereabouts secret. If I was to keep that pledge, I couldn't tell Tom or Taylor where he was. I liked Jimi. He hadn't been a thief all his life. He'd been a hardworking husband and father. When the home life went sour on him, he'd taken his chance. He simply transferred a bunch of money that he was holding in offshore accounts for various criminal types into his own accounts. He disappeared, newly wealthy with no obligations to anyone. I was, so far, the only one of his victims with the wherewithal to find him.

His phone rang five times and went to voicemail.

"It's me, Breeze," I said. "You're not in danger yet, but I can make that happen real fast if you don't call me back immediately."

He called back within thirty seconds.

"I don't like the tone of the message you just left me, Breeze," he said. "What's going on?"

"You ever heard of Tom Melendez?" I asked.

"I don't like this at all," he said. "He was the money man for a certain investor I dealt with. His boss would probably like to find me."

"Tom ran off," I said. "His boss wanted to find him first. I took the job."

"How in the hell did you get involved in that?" he asked.

"Taylor," I said. "She was getting some serious pressure about all the missing money. She was the one who hired me. I trusted her. Now I'm not so sure."

"What do you mean by that?" he asked.

"It wasn't a retrieval," I said. "It was a hit job. They want Tom dead. I'm sure they'll get around to looking for you sooner or later."

"He's not dead?" he asked.

"Not yet," I answered. "I have him though. How do we call off the hit, Jimi?"

"How should I know?" he said. "I'm not a mobster."

"Can you put the money back in the man's account?" I asked. "That should do it."

"Christ, Breeze," he said. "You already cost me a half-million."

"We're talking about a man's life, Jimi," I said. "You should have thought about that when you decided to become a thief. Taylor could still get into deep shit over this, maybe dead. I'm out here running around the Bahamas trying to stay alive. Pay it back Jimi."

"Okay, okay," he said. "But just what Tom gave me. I'll have to take my chances with the rest of them. You haven't given anyone any clues to where I am, have you?"

"No. I haven't said a word," I said. "But remember, if I need you to help, I know where you are. I know who to tell as well. You might consider relocation."

"You're probably right," he said. "I'll call you back to confirm when the transfer is complete."

I explained to Holly what was going on. I put the dinghy in the water so I could tell Tom. The money would magically reappear in the appropriate account. Hopefully, the hunt for Tom, Breeze, and Jimi D. would end. I'd soothe Holly's feeling in the Bahamian sun. We'd make love in the moonlight and live happily ever after, or not.

Tom was ecstatic. Holly was still a bit peeved.

"So you managed to weasel your way out of this one," Holly said. "Seems like your life would be a whole lot easier if you just avoided this kind of shit in the first place."

"What can I say?" I said. "Chicks dig a dangerous man, until the danger hits close to home."

"Don't be clever with me, Breeze," she said. "That was bullshit. You didn't come close to thinking it through. You didn't consider the consequences. If you did, then you were willing to let that man die just so you could fulfill your mission."

"I didn't think it through," I admitted. "I thought I was helping Taylor. I never thought she'd put me in that situation. I thought I knew her better."

"She must have been as good in bed as she is pretty," she said. "Rotted your brain."

I was at a loss for witty comebacks. I'd been a little too sure of myself. Holly had humbled me. She made me realize that I wasn't always as smart as I thought I was. Taylor had played me like a fiddle and I never saw it coming. I looked at Holly. There was no deception with her. She was exactly who she appeared to be. She wasn't a brilliant lawyer. She wasn't a fashion model, but she was real. I couldn't regret bringing her on this trip, but I could regret putting her in harm's way.

"I'm sorry," I said. "I was a dumbass. I appreciate how much you've helped. I'm glad that you are here, but I'm sorry it got so screwed up."

"Let's ditch this dude and run naked on the beach," she said with a smile.

Jimi called back to confirm the money transfer. I took Holly's phone over to Tom's boat. He hadn't arranged to make calls in the Bahamas. He thought his American phone would work. He made the call to his former boss. He waited while the accounts were looked up. The money was there. Tom made it sound like he'd recovered the money himself. It went missing. He went to find it. It was back. Tom was the hero. The hit was called off. There was just the wasted twenty-five grand given to me left to deal with. I told Tom to assure him that it would be paid back. We were off the hook.

I called Taylor.

"The situation has been resolved," I told her. "But not in the manner that you expected."

"What's that supposed to mean?" she asked. "What's going on, Breeze?"

"Your former client has his money back," I said. "Tom Melendez is still alive."

"How'd you manage that?" she asked. "You're amazing."

"I don't want to hear how amazing I am," I said. "I'm not in the mood to be flattered by you."

"Breeze, what's wrong?" she asked. "It all worked out for the best, thanks to you."

"You set me up," I said. "And now you owe me."

"How would I owe you?" she asked. "I got you fifty grand."

"You only got me twenty-five," I said. "I didn't earn the rest. Now I have to pay back what you gave me. I want you to give your client twenty-five grand on my behalf. I want it done immediately, like today."

"Why would I pay the money back?" she asked. "We had a deal and you didn't keep it."

"Because if you don't, I'll burn you down," I said. "You bribed a judge with my money, remember? I'll spill it all. You'll be indicted. You'll lose your license. Your life will be over."

"If you confess to that," she said. "You'll go to jail."

"No I won't," I said. "I'll go on the run. You don't know where I am right now. No one will ever find me either. You know I can do it. You'll be stuck paying the price. I'll be drinking rum somewhere in the sun."

"Fuck you, Meade Breeze," she said. "You bastard. We had something together once."

"I thought so too, Taylor," I said. "Pay the man the money."

"I'll pay him," she said. "When will I see you again?"

"You won't," I said. "Goodbye, Taylor."

I hung up before she could reply. I handed the phone back to Holly.

"That book is closed," I said.

"You okay?" Holly asked.

"If you weren't here, I might be a little sad, too be honest with you," I said. "But we've got beaches to walk and sunsets to watch."

"Glad I could be of assistance," she said. "How do we ditch the Bat Cave?"

I spent a few hours plotting courses on Tom's GPS. He could get fuel at Chub Cay, which was just around the corner, or he could continue south to Nassau. I put in routes back to Miami from either location. I taught him how to make his own routes if he found the need. He asked what our plans were, hinting that he'd like to tag along.

"This has got to be where we part ways," I told him. "No offense, but I'd like to be alone with Holly."

"I don't blame you," he said. "She's an interesting chick."

"Are we good, you and me?" I asked. "Sorry for the ugliness back at the marina."

"You saved my ass, man," he said. "If you hadn't gotten the money back, I'd either be dead or on the run for the rest of my life. I don't think I would have lasted very long out there on my own."

"Good luck to you," I said. "Go home. Live a normal life."

"Thanks, brother," he said. "Stay safe."

# Six

"Mission accomplished, sort of," said Holly. "What do we do next?"

"I would like to hold you prisoner on this boat," I said. "I will force you to walk white sand beaches, swim in warm blue waters, and drink too much rum. Or we can make arrangements to get you back to your boat. Your call."

"The first option sounds very appealing," she said. "But I will have to get my boat one of these days."

"Just say the word," I said. "We can fly down there and I'll help you bring it back to Florida. Whatever you want to do."

"Those islands we passed on the way here sure looked nice," she said.

"You want to go check them out?" I asked.

"Could take months to explore them all," she said with a sly grin.

"I've got all the time in the world," I said. "No more missions."

"No more missions," she said. "At least not for a while."

In my bunk that night, I tried to think about the future. It was something I seldom did. I lived for today, maybe tomorrow. That was it. Now, my future stretched out in front of me. It was an empty void that I should probably fill. I had money. I was free from the long arm of the law. I'd burnt my bridge with Taylor. Jimi D. was very likely to relocate and never answer my calls again. I'd spread the last of my dead wife's ashes once and for all. I could do anything. I could go anywhere. I had no idea what direction to take.

I thought that Holly was a special person. I did not feel that we would make a life together though. She was missing something in her life. Something was broken, that only she could fix. I could listen. I could be her friend. I'd certainly volunteer to be her sex partner if she chose, but I couldn't be responsible for making her whole. It was something she must work out herself. On the other hand, if she wasn't a lost soul, she probably wouldn't be lost in the Bahamas with a boat bum like me. Being a rogue had its advantages. I told myself that shit would work out, just like it had done with Tom. Just like it always did.

The following morning, we retraced our path back up the Berry Islands chain. We re-entered the inside route at Market Fish Cay. We passed the spot where we'd anchored with Tom and continued south to the backside of Hoffman Cay. I found a beach cove at the southern end of the island and set the anchor in eight feet of water. There were no other boats in sight. The scenery was awe-inspiring. We settled on the back deck with beers in hand to await the sunset.

I almost spit out my beer when Holly broke the silence.

"I haven't been laid in over two years," she said. "I ought to be horny as hell right about now."

"But you're not?" I asked.

"I think I am," she said. "A little bit. I'm just worried that it won't go right. I'm overly self-conscious I guess."

"When I first met you," I said. "I thought you were kind of attractive in a funky sort of way. Now that we've been together this long, I think you're hot as hell."

"It's weird isn't it?" she asked.

"What's weird?" I said.

"When we first met, I thought you were okay looking for an older guy," she said. "Now I think you're pretty damn good looking."

"I guess we grew on each other," I said.

"Without getting on each other's nerves," she said.

"I like you, Holly," I said.

"I like you too, Breeze," she said.

"Do you want to have sex?" I asked.

"That was real romantic," she said.

"Straight to the point," I said.

"Let's do it," she said. "I've been avoiding it long enough."

Suddenly, I was the self-conscious one. I hadn't had sex in quite a while either. Was it with

Taylor? I wanted it to be good with Holly. It was no time for performance anxiety. She took of her top and dropped her shorts. The lace undies remained. I took off my shirt and dropped my shorts. The boxers remained. We moved in close and kissed. I took her hand and led her to my bunk. I slid her panties down to the floor and motioned her to the bed. I shed the boxers and joined her. We were both a little awkward at first. I decided to go down on her, in fear that it would be over too fast. This turned out to be a successful tactic. Only when I was sure that she was satisfied did I enter her. It was slow and gentle at first. I took her cues to pick up the pace. She urged me on, telling me to go ahead and let go. The awkwardness was gone. There was nothing to fear or be ashamed about. We were just two lost boat bums sharing a closeness. We fulfilled the needs of our bodies, if not our souls. I was grateful.

"God, thank you, Breeze," she said. "That was nice. I worried it wouldn't be. It was good."

"Trust me," I said. "The pleasure was all mine. I'm pretty happy right now."

"Happy is good," she said. "Let's just be happy."

"Deal."

We stayed happy for another month. We explored every beach and island trail between Hoffman Cay and Whale Cay. We hiked to the Blue Hole and dove into its spectacular depths. We caught fish for dinner. Holly dove for lobster. We drank our drinks at sunset every night. Occasionally, we returned to my bed. It was never white-hot fireworks, full of crying passion, but it was always satisfying. We were kind lovers, attending to each other's needs, unselfish. We didn't analyze it. We were just happy.

At the end of the month, we were running out of fresh water and other necessities, like toilet paper. We headed back to the marina at Great Harbor Cay to re-provision. I hoped it wouldn't be the end of Holly's stay.

Hans was waiting as we pulled into our slip. He did not look happy to see us. He stood with his arms crossed. His dock hands assisted, but he stood frozen. Once we were tied up, I hopped onto the dock to greet him.

"What's up, Hans?" I asked. "You're lacking your usual cheer."

"You left in the middle of the night," he said.

"We had sort of an emergency," I said.

"There is the matter of your unpaid bill, Mr. Breeze," he said.

"Oh shit, Hans," I said. "I'm so sorry. I'll pay it, plus interest if necessary. Long story."

We walked together up to the marina office. Once inside, I pulled a wad of hundreds out of my pocket and made good on my bill. Hans loosened up after that.

"Did your emergency have something to do with Mr. Melendez?" he asked.

"Yes it did," I answered. "You don't have to believe me, but it was a matter of life and death. I wouldn't have run out on you otherwise."

"He didn't pay his bill either," said Hans.

"I'll take care of it right now," I said. "How much?"

He told me and I pulled off more hundreds to give to him. We'd been there ten minutes and my pocket money had disappeared. Marinas are good for that. Hans then wanted to know how long we would stay. He wanted the payment up front. I couldn't blame him. I had to return to the boat to get more cash. I paid for a week in advance. We needed some time to get groceries and give the boat a good going over.

Holly handed me a beer as soon as I returned.

"I liked it better out there in the wilderness," she said. "There's people here. Feels weird."

"Our naked sunbathing habit will have to be put on hold," I said.

"Just don't drag me to another one of those potluck dinners," she said.

"We'll just take care of our business and head out," I said. "Necessary evil."

Our month in the sun had turned us both deep brown. We had even erased our tan lines. My hair had gone from dirty brown to pure blond. I'd gotten leaner due to the steady diet of fish and lobster. Holly's dreads were almost pure white. When she undid them and let her hair down, darker blonde streaks showed through. I liked her hair down. It made her look more feminine. When we were freshly showered we'd make love to clean bodies. I'd run my fingers through her loose hair, even give it a tug now and then. Afterwards, she always put it back in dreads.

There was no longer a hint of awkwardness between us. We'd overcome our initial modesty. Our lovemaking was no more frequent, but it was more adventurous. We talked about all manner of things openly and freely. That month had been as close to bliss as I could imagine. Still, we had no commitment. We avoided telling each other that we were in love. We didn't even discuss it. We just avoided the topic. Neither of us had completely opened our hearts. Our friendship was deep and real, but our love affair was missing something. We weren't willing to put ourselves on the line and admit to deeper feelings. I was waiting for her. Maybe she was waiting for me. Maybe neither of us truly felt it. In the meantime, we were partners. I would have taken a bullet to save her life. I did everything in my power to provide happiness for her. We were enjoying a strange life together. We vowed to make the best of it, as long as it lasted.

Over the next few days, we re-provisioned and ran through our list of maintenance duties. *Leap of Faith* got her first good washing in months. We declined an offer from the locals to attend Sunday church service. We took advantage of the opportunity to buy lunch from *The Conch Salad* man, who set up at the end of the dock. We loved the fresh Bahamian bread that came around the marina. The people were friendly. The facility was nice, but we felt out of place. Both Holly and I quickly longed for a return to solitude.

We discussed our options over beers at happy hour. South of Nassau the Exumas beckoned. To our north called the Abacos. A side trip to the Eleutheras wasn't out of the question. We went through the guide books and Explorer Charts together. The possibilities were endless. Our only worry would be hurricanes come summer. When I brought up hurricanes, Holly realized her boat was still left alone down in Grand Cayman.

"I've got to do something about my boat," she said. "I can't just leave it there forever."

I hadn't mentioned her boat even though it had been on my mind. A trip to retrieve it was a good excuse for her to leave me, maybe for good. If I went with her, I could still persuade her to continue through the islands with me afterwards.

"I'll help move it," I said. "Where do we take it?"

"I don't know," she said. "There's really nothing for me in Florida. What am I going to do? Get a job? Stay in one place forever?"

"You've earned some money in this deal," I said. "You can survive for a while."

"We have to refigure the split," she said. "You didn't get the whole fifty. What's a third of twenty-five?"

"I'll give you half," I offered. "We're partners now."

"Thanks," she said. "But even that won't last forever."

"Listen, Holly," I began. "I know we haven't broached the subject, but I don't want you to leave. Let's figure out what to do with your boat. Then let's figure out where to go next, together."

"That's sweet, Breeze," she said. "I'm not ready to give this up either, but I can never give up my boat. You understand right?"

"Of course, I do," I said. "Our boats are our life."

"So what do we do with mine?" she asked.

"What about bringing it here?" I said. "We'll fly to it and sail her back. *Leap of Faith* will be safe here while we're gone. Your boat will be safe here when we travel south."

"What about taking my boat south?" she said. "We'll be paying for a slip either way. Cheaper to sail."

"I'll have to think about that," I said. "You know I'm no sailor."

"You've taught me a lot," she said. "I'll teach you to sail. You'll love it."

So we changed our plans. We'd fly to Grand Cayman and sail Holly's boat back to Great Harbor. We'd dicker over which boat to take south during our journey. I really didn't want to give up my vessel, but I would if it meant Holly would stay with me. The marina at Great Harbor was a good hurricane hole. She'd be safe if I had to leave her there. I walked up to the office to get Han's advice for our travel plans.

"I can arrange a boat to take you to Freeport," he said. "You can get a flight from there."

"I'll pay for dockage as far in advance as you need to be comfortable," I said.

"We will take good care of your boat while you're gone," he said. "No worries."

"Thanks, Hans," I said. "I'm sorry about our earlier mix-up."

"I'd like to talk to you about that a little more, if I may," he said.

"Shoot," I said.

"The day we woke up to find you gone," he said. "Three men came to the marina asking for Mr. Melendez. They asked for you too. They were not boaters or businessmen. They wore shoulder holsters. They were obviously trouble. We won't tolerate trouble here at Great Harbor."

"That trouble is behind us now," I told him. "I made sure that nothing went down in your marina. We got tipped off that these men were coming. The situation has since been resolved, peacefully."

"What exactly is your line of work, Breeze?" he asked. "You're too young to be retired."

"I do odd jobs from time to time," I said. "I came here to get Tom Melendez, but the situation changed. I ended up helping him out of trouble."

"I sensed as much," he said. "You must have hidden talents, to do this kind of work."

"I've decided to get out of that type of business," I said. "Holly and I just want to be left alone."

"She's quite the young lady," he said. "A refreshing change from the blue hairs we so often see here."

"I thank my lucky stars every day she sticks around," I said.

"As you should," he said. "Now have a safe trip. We look forward to your return."

"Thanks again, Hans," I said.

I felt bad about causing a stir for Hans. I liked him. Everyone in the community, both locals and boaters, respected him. He did a fine job as caretaker of his little slice of paradise. He was kind and genuine. I swore to keep a low profile whenever I was in his marina in the future. I couldn't afford to lose his good will.

Holly was working with the chart plotter when I got back. She was trying to lay a course from Grand Cayman to Great Harbor. She wasn't happy that the machine wouldn't draw curves. The big half-circle around Cuba was giving her fits.

"I can make that a lot easier for you," I said.

"Okay, smart guy," she said. "What am I doing wrong?"

"Picking the wrong course to begin with," I said. "There is already an old track to Marathon. We just stop off there for provisions and then cross to the Gulf Stream."

"That'll add like a whole day," she said.

"It will be much cheaper to get food and fuel in the states," I said. "We'll be on familiar waters. We'll have shelter if the weather turns. We'll have internet too. It's the prudent choice."

"Now, all of the sudden, Mr. Seat of his Pants wants to be prudent," she laughed.

"I just want to get us back here in one piece," I said.

"We'll do it your way," she said. "But remember, once we get on my boat, I'm the captain."

"Aye, aye," I said, saluting.

# Seven

In order to fly from Freeport in the Bahamas to Grand Cayman, one had to change planes in Miami. One also had to pay five hundred bucks for the privilege. One also needed a credit card, to make a reservation, which neither of us had. I brought the problem up with Hans, who assured me that many people paid cash for plane tickets in Freeport. I'd just have to show up and hope two seats were available on the next flight. Thank God, they were.

I hated Miami airport. Adding Customs and Immigration to the process made it even more difficult. By the time we cleared security I needed a beer. It only cost me eight bucks. The second leg of the trip was mercifully short and uneventful. I'd rather sail across an ocean than fly across one any day. We landed on Grand Cayman in the middle of the afternoon. We both knew our way around the island, but neither of us wanted to walk. If I owned a cell phone, I'd have my cabbie friend Theo's number. Holly was on it, though. She looked up the number via Google or whatever and we made the call. I specifically requested Theo.

He rolled up fast and skidded to a stop. His old Chevy let out a cloud of smoke and the smell of burning rubber. He still had dreadlocks, but all the baubles were gone. He was clean shaven. He didn't smell like dope.

"My old friend, Breeze," he said, extending his hand. "I never would have thought it. What brings you back to my island?"

"This is my friend Holly," I said. "We came to get her boat, sail it back to the Bahamas."

"If we could all live like you, Breeze," he chuckled. "Globetrotting playboy off on another adventure."

"You look well, my friend," I told him. "Life is good I hope."

"My wife loves me again," he said. "My little girl loves me. Everybody loves Theo these days."

"I'm glad to hear it," I said.

"After you come here the first time," he said. "I straighten up and fly right. I quit the ganja. I cleaned up and worked hard. I come home to my family every night. The money gave us a little boost, mon. Now I don't spend it on dope no more."

"That's great, man," I said. "I'm real happy for you."

"You gonna stay a while?" he asked. "Come see my family."

"I'd love to, but we have to get to Holly's boat," I said. "I might want to look up Jimi D. while we're here, though."

"I been keeping an eye on that dude since you left," he said. "Split town the other day. Just up and gone."

"I'm not surprised," I said. "We've had more business since I left here."

"I'm sure you came out on top," he said. "Smartest man I ever did meet."

"It worked out, Theo," I said.

Theo dropped us at Holly's boat and we said our goodbyes. I gave him a fifty on a five dollar fare and told him to keep the change. He didn't argue. Her vessel was tied up at a private dock. No one had touched it since she'd left. It was covered in bird shit. Cobwebs hung from the rigging. The topsides were turning green from neglect. I thought Holly was going to cry.

"I'll help clean her up like it was my own," I told her.

"You bet your ass you will," she said. "Start with those spider webs. I hate those things."

I grabbed a stick and started winding up webs. By the time I finished, it looked like cotton candy. I tossed it overboard. Holly opened up the hatches. The musty smell of mildew wafted about the deck. We had our work cut out for us.

"Let's let her air out," I said. "Go get something to eat first."

"Good idea," she said. "It's pretty rank down there."

"At least it's still floating," I joked.

"It's mechanically sound, Breeze," she said. "Your boat would look a mess too if you left it alone for a couple months."

"No doubt," I said.

I worried that the state of her vessel would cause her to not want to leave it again. I worried that the same thing would happen to my vessel if we left it behind. We hadn't come to terms on which boat to use. I didn't bring it up over dinner.

We slept in the cockpit that night. The cabin and bunks needed some serious cleaning to make them habitable. The next day we picked up all the cleaning supplies we could carry and got to work. Holly scrubbed the interior with white vinegar. I sloshed a lethal combination of soap and bleach all over the decks and took a brush to them. We cleaned all day without taking a break. I was covered in sweat and smelled of bleach. Holly was covered in sweat and smelled like vinegar. I had black grime on my knees and elbows. Holly had green grime under her fingernails and even in her hair.

We sat drinking a beer and soaking in our filth when the day was done. Holly leaned down to scrub some gunk off of her toes. When she came up, I was there to plant a kiss on her lips, grime and all. She laughed.

"You still think I'm hot?" she said, spinning around to reveal the full extent of her dirtiness.

"I'm turned on by green hair," I said.

"Admit it, Breeze," she said. "You're really into me."

"I never said I wasn't."

"Never said you were, either," she replied. "But look at you. You're halfway around the world scrubbing some chick's filthy boat. You paid a thousand bucks to get us here. I look like total shit and you give me a kiss. The evidence is clear."

"Ok then, I'm really into you," I said.

"Ha," she said. "I knew it."

"Well?" I asked.

"Well what" she asked back.

"You just gonna leave me hanging?"

"Silly Breeze," she said. "You know I'm into you. You think I would have left my boat here to get like this if I wasn't?"

"I don't know," I said. "We haven't talked about it."

"Because neither one of us is comfortable talking about it," she said. "We'll think it to death and suck all the fun out of it."

"Wouldn't want that to happen," I said. "Just be happy, right?"

"Exactly," she said. "Now let's get cleaned up before you try to kiss me again."

We took deck showers in our bathing suits. Holly was a sight all soaped up in her tight bikini. After our little chat, I really wanted to do her right there on deck for all to see, but she wouldn't have it. The vinegar smell down below was still overpowering. We waited until after dark, and made quiet, sneaky love under a blanket in the cockpit. It was awesome. I felt that we'd really crossed a new bridge in our relationship. I slept the sleep of the world's most contented man.

The interior space smelled a lot better in the morning. There was still work to be done, but we could live with it the way it was. After breakfast, Holly dove in to clean the bottom. I raised the sails to air them out and inspect them. I didn't really know what I was looking for, but they looked okay to me. When Holly was done, we ran the engine long enough to bring it to operating temperature. It sounded fine. We'd have a two-day shake down run to Marathon. Anything that needed fixing could be addressed there.

We picked up enough groceries to get us to Florida. I was already missing the fresh fish and lobster that we'd enjoyed in the Bahamas. After dinner, we started looking at the weather forecast. As a trawler owner, I look for calm winds to make a passage. On a sailboat, you need wind to make you move. You'd prefer favorable winds. All the sailors I knew constantly complained. It's too windy. It's not windy enough. The wind is in the wrong direction. Holly's boat was big and heavy. It performed best with a pretty good wind in her sails. Twenty knots of wind was nothing for her. I wouldn't take my boat out in twenty knot winds, if I had a choice. Good wind meant waves. She assured me that she knew what she was doing. Her vessel didn't even get up to speed until the wind hit twenty knots. Fifteen was still light winds for her. I preferred ten or less on my boat, though I'd been through much worse.

The next day's forecast called for light winds. We'd burn too much fuel motoring out into the open ocean. The following day it was supposed to pick up out of the west at fifteen knots. There was a little ripple of a disturbance between Cuba and the Florida Keys that might complicate things. It looked like a small area of really tight gradients that meant high winds, but it only covered a dozen or so miles of the straits. It was her call and we were going the following day.

We spent the off day continuing to tidy up the boat. We secured things even better than we'd done on my trawler. Sailboats heeled over under sail. Things would fall even under ideal conditions. We double checked oil and coolant levels. We inspected lines and rigging. We triple checked the weather. That little irregularity was still out there. It hadn't grown or moved. The winds would hold at fifteen to twenty out of the west. A nice point of sail, Holly informed me.

"How's it feel to be the mate and not the captain?" she asked.

"This is worse than when you were on my boat," I said. "I'm lost in all this rigging. Tell me what to do and I'll try not to screw up."

She ran through some terminology to get me acquainted. She told me what rope was a line and what line was a sheet. Back stay, fore stay, spreaders and reefs, it was all foreign to me. She pointed out the telltales on the sails that told her what the wind was doing. She had a small compass and a small GPS mounted in front of the wheel. I could barely make out the marks on the little device.

The time came to go and we untied from the dock. Holly motored us out through the harbor and pointed us into the wind. I held us steady while she raised the main. It filled with wind and we lurched ahead. The boat heeled to starboard a bit. Holly came back to the wheel and we fell off with the wind and increased speed. The boat righted itself. She put up a jib and we increased speed some more. She made a few adjustments before returning to the wheel. The engine was shut down. She corrected our course, and turned to me with a big smile. We were flying.

"Isn't this great?" she squealed.

I had to admit it was pretty cool. There was nothing but the sound of the wind and the hull slicing through the waves.

"Feel it, Breeze," she yelled. "Feel the energy."

I could feel it. The boat harnessed the power of the wind and came to life. I felt like a tiny jockey riding a great thoroughbred. We galloped through the waves. Holly was electrified. She couldn't contain her joy. She laughed and whooped at the wind. She danced a jig in the cockpit. She took off her bikini top and held it up like a flag in the breeze. After a minute, she let it go. It flew off behind us and fell into the sea.

"Come on, Breeze," she said. "You gotta get into it. Let yourself go. Enjoy it."

I was enjoying it, but I wasn't sharing in the religious experience that she was having. I could see it in her eyes. They were ablaze. I could see it in the lightness of her movements. She was one with her ship. She lived to sail. She was free at last.

"I'm loving that you're so happy," I said.

"You ain't seen nothing yet," she said. "Come here."

When I reached her, she leapt on to me. She wrapped her legs around my waist and her hands around my neck. I almost fell backwards. She covered my neck in passionate kisses. I slowly lowered us to the deck, where she literally ripped off my shirt. Sailing had ignited her passion. We had that animal sex that new lovers had. It was no holds barred, down and dirty, pure lust. She caught me off guard at first, but I recovered quickly. I let myself go too. I matched her every decadent move. We fell into the rhythm of the boats movement over the waves. She was a goddess and I was Adonis.

We ruled the seven seas and each other's bodies. It was a mind blowing, spiritual experience.

We laid there when it was over, trying to catch our breath. We stared up at the sky, the clouds and the telltales on the sails.

"We'll have to go sailing more often," I said. "You were unbelievable."

"Best ever," she said. "I've been underestimating you all this time."

"Wow."

"Yeah, wow."

# Eight

We ran into that little disturbance in the Florida Straits. It hit us almost without warning. By the time we felt a change in the air, it was on us. We scrambled for life vests and safety harnesses.

"Pull the jib in," Holly yelled. "I'll reef the main."

As I began lowering the forward sail, it began flapping wildly. It beat me about the head and shoulders for a few minutes before I could get it under control. It wasn't pretty, but it was wound up and secured. Holly had shortened her sail significantly, but it still seemed like too much to me. The winds were pushing fifty knots and it had begun to rain horizontally.

"Why don't you fire the engine and bring the rest of the main down?" I asked.

"You're thinking like a power boater," she said. "This is a sailing vessel."

That's when the thunder and lightning made it presence known. I had to admit being a little nervous. That tall mast looked like a fine lightning rod to me. I was pretty sure we were going to get fried at any minute. It turned out that we had bigger problems to worry about. A freak wind gust was the culprit. It was like a rogue wave of hammering wind. It slammed us over and onto our side. It felt like the fist of Thor, reaching down from the heavens to smite us. The top half of the mast was in the water. The port side rail was under the surface far enough to allow the sea to enter the open companionway door.

The deep, full keel did its job. As fast as the boat went over, it righted itself. Starboard side shrouds popped free and lashed about like Kraken tentacles. They tried to pry the chain plates loose before they tore free. The mast wobbled at first, then snapped. The remaining mainsail, shrouds and mast went over the side in a violent tangle, taking out the safety lines. Stanchions ripped out of the toe rail and went overboard with the rest of the mess. It was all still attached in various places, threatening to pull us over again.

I'd been frozen in place after the initial shock. I had managed not to fall overboard or get sliced by flying rigging. Holly was huddled below the wheel with her arms over her head. She looked unhurt.

"Bolt cutters," I yelled. "We've got to cut that stuff free."

She nodded and began to crawl towards the companionway. Her safety harness stopped her short. She cursed and untethered herself. She came back up with the bolt cutters.

"There's a lot of water down there," she said.

I used a seat cushion like a shield, blocking the occasional sword swipe of the swinging rigging. One by one I cut through shrouds and stays until the whole threatening glob sunk below the waves. I sunk to my hands and knees, watching blood drip to the deck. The battle had lasted five minutes or less, but I was exhausted. I looked up at what remained of the mast. It had sheared off just above the spreaders. It rocked from side to side with each roll of the waves. I didn't think it would stay up for long with nothing to support it. *Fugging sailboats,* I thought to myself. Sailing had suddenly lost its charm for me.

Holly was below making sure the pumps were working. They were. She didn't cry or appear to be in shock. She was doing what had to be done. We need the engine to run now, and keeping water away from it was job one. When the water first came in, it was knee deep in the salon. It took a while for it to work its way into the bilge so the pumps could remove it. We looked at each other, then back out the open companionway. The wind had died. The rain had stopped. The thunder was distant. We climbed back on deck to survey the damage. We'd gone through a very intense storm, but it had been very small in size. That one fatal blow was later determined to be a micro burst. It had only affected a mile or so of the open ocean. We just happened to be in its kill zone.

Holly's boat was hurt pretty badly. I was still worried about the mast.

"Any ideas?" she asked.

"Maybe," I said. "Get the engine started. I'll rig something up."

She went to check the water levels before attempting to start the engine. I dug through some lines to find the longest ones. I coiled up half and hurled it up at the port spreader. It took three tries before I got it up and over. I tied it off loosely to a port cleat. I repeated the process on the starboard side. I moved back and forth slowly adding tension until the mast stiffened up. Holly saw what I was doing and went below. She returned with two one-hundred foot lines. We went through the whole thing again to secure the mast from fore to aft. It looked like hell, but it seemed to work. We weren't going to sail the damn thing. We just didn't want it to come crashing down on us before we could make safe harbor.

The engine started, and stayed running. I pumped my fist in the air in Holly's direction. She gave me a thumbs up. Then I saw her smack the side of the GPS. It wasn't working. She tried the VHF radio. It was dead too. Saltwater had gotten in somewhere it shouldn't be and killed the electronics. I fiddled with wires and fuses to no avail.

"Breeze, you're bleeding pretty bad," she said.

I looked down for blood and didn't see any.

"Your back," she said. "Your shirt is soaked in blood."

I couldn't see it, and until then I hadn't felt it. Now that I was aware, it started to sting.

"We've got to stop the bleeding," she said.

"Get us headed towards the Keys," I said. "We'll hit one of them. I'll get the first aid kit."

I went below and my knees buckled. I started to feel light-headed. I had just enough sense to yell for Holly before I fell to the floor. I laid there and watched a pool of blood grow around me.

"Shit, Breeze," Holly said. "It's bad."

She was tearing bandages open with her teeth and pushing them into the wound. She had blood all over her hands.

"Don't pass out on me," she said. "I need help getting this boat home. I can't lose my boat, Breeze. And I can't lose you."

"Stop, bleeding," I mumbled.

"I'm trying damn it," she yelled.

"Duct tape," I said. "Tape it up."

She left my side. I just laid there like a brick. I was aware, but my body wasn't cooperating. I couldn't move. I was too weak to even speak again. I had a vague notion that she had returned and was working on me, then I was out.

I was still the floor, facedown, when I came to. There were piles of bloody bandages all around me. I tried to look around. I couldn't see Holly, but I heard her voice.

"I didn't want to try to move you," she said. "The duct tape did the trick. It's still seeping out a little, but it's mostly stopped."

"Help me," I said. "Up."

She was able to get me into a sitting position. She told me to hold still. More bandages went over the wound and medical tape went around my chest.

"That's going to hurt when it come off," I said.

"You've got bigger problems," she said. "We need to get you to a hospital."

"Marathon," I said. "Hospital there."

"I'm not sure I can find it," she said. "I'm sorry, Breeze. I'm not sure where we are."

"Paper chart," I said.

She brought the chart to me. I asked her to point to where she thought we were when the storm hit. She pointed to a spot about forty miles north of Havana. I asked for our current course. She told me we were headed northeast. Our speed was five knots. We'd been motoring for two hours. I used my finger to draw a line ten miles to the northeast. I pointed.

"We're here," I said. "Current course takes us just east of Key West. Take us about ten degrees more east."

"Okay," she said. "I see what you're doing."

"If you can get me up there with you," I said. "I know all the landmarks. I can guide you in."

"I can't miss the Seven Mile Bridge," she said. "Goofball."

"Oh yeah, sorry," I said. "I'll just rest here. Can you get me on the settee?"

She woke me up hours later. Once I sat up, I felt a little better. My head was clear. I wanted to go out on deck to assist her if I could. She wouldn't have it. It was her boat and she damn well knew how to drop anchor by herself. I was in no shape to argue. I felt so bad for her. Her boat was a wreck. I was no help. She'd have to be the strong one.

I laid face down and felt the throbbing pain in my back. I counted heart beats. I made it to twenty-five before I was out again. I woke up in Fisherman's Hospital in Marathon. The first face I saw was Holly's. She looked like hell. I assumed I looked even worse.

"The nurses weren't too happy with my duct tape repair," she said.

"What did they replace it with?" I asked.

"Staples," she said. "A whole bunch of them. You've got a railroad track from your shoulder to the middle of your back."

"Your boat?" I asked.

"Anchored by the bridge," she said. "It's in real bad shape, Breeze."

"We'll make her new," I said. "I promise."

"You just worry about healing up," she said. "I don't know which is busted up worse, you or my boat."

"Go find Howie, at the Marathon Boat Yard," I told her. "Tell him I sent you. He's the guy who fixed up *Miss Leap*."

"It's going to cost a fortune," she said.

"I don't care," I said. "Tell him same deal as last time. Only the best people and the best materials. I'll be over to see him as soon as I can."

"I'll talk to him," she said. "But you lay there and rest."

I rested for three days. The fluids and painkillers did their thing. I started walking around, dragging that stand with the bags hanging from it. I peed on my own. After five days they let me go free. I'd have to come back in another two weeks to have the staples removed. I wondered if I could get Holly to yank them out with some pliers. She brought a duffel bag full of cash to settle up my bill with the hospital. They didn't blink an eye. You'd have thought they got a hundred grand in cash every day. Such was life in the Keys.

Holly and I went to see Howie at the boatyard. It had been three or four years since I'd dealt with him. He'd taken a special interest in my boat. He supervised her complete restoration. I'd left and run off to the BVI's on my own personal mission. When I returned, Howie had taken my last few dollars to get her out of hock. It had been worth it. All the work was exceptional. *Leap of Faith* had been transformed into the finest vessel in its class. I didn't have the heart to tell him about all the bullet holes she's suffered afterwards.

"Breeze, you old sea dog, you," said Howie. "I hope your boat isn't as busted up as this young ladies is. I'll not stand you mistreating her."

"The girl or the boat? You damn Yankee," I said.

"Neither one, you boat bum," he said. "Looks like you were pretty rough on both of them getting here."

"It was my fault," interrupted Holly. "I was the captain."

"What you done wrong, Miss, was bring along this scalawag," said Howie.

"Can you save it?" I asked.

"What kind of question is that?" snorted Howie. "Of course I can. If you got enough money, I can turn it into a Rolls Royce."

"I just want it back the way it was," said Holly. "I can't afford Rolls Royce."

Howie looked at me and wouldn't release his stare. He was trying to figure out if I had a bunch of cash or not. You could never tell with me. One day I had a pile. The next day it was all gone. A full rehab of Holly's boat would put a significant dent in my current cash supply.

"Let's do it up right, Howie," I said. "Give her full treatment."

"Breeze, I can't do that," said Holly.

"I can," I said. "I know how much that boat means to you. I don't want it half-assed."

"Ain't nothing half-ass around here, buddy," said Howie.

"Ain't nothing cheap either," I replied. "Can we stay on it for a while in the yard?"

"Absolutely not," said Howie. "I know we let you do that before. But the rules have changed. I can't risk breaking them. Sorry."

"Don't sweat it," I said. "Just take good care of her."

"Leave it to me," he said. "Come back in a couple months, maybe three. Good as new I swear."

There we were, homeless in the Keys. My boat was far, far away. Holly's boat wasn't getting us back to it anytime soon. Any argument about which boat to use in the Bahamas had been rendered mute.

"What now?" Holly asked.

"We figure out how to get a flight back to Freeport," I said. "Then we get a boat back to Great Harbor."

"Simple as that," she said. "Start figuring."

We took the Lower Keys shuttle to the Key West Airport. Flights left for Fort Lauderdale on a regular basis. We dodged the roosters in the parking lot and approached the one and only terminal for ticket information. We paid cash for the next flight out. We paid ten dollars each for rum drinks. Holly informed me that I had tiny red spots dotting the back of my shirt.

"Should have left the duct tape on," I said.

We used the men's room for a nurse's station. Holly cleaned me up and put some bandages over it. I dug a clean shirt out of my duffel bag. I got very tired waiting for the plane.

"Maybe we should have waited before we traveled," she said.

"We didn't have a place to stay," I said. "I'll be all right. I'm just tired."

She took my head and laid it on her shoulder. She had to wake me when they called our flight. The trip to Lauderdale was a short one. We had to fight with the customer service agent because we wanted to pay cash. After getting a manager involved, we got our boarding passes. I was asleep before we left the ground. Holly woke me again just before we landed in Freeport. I did not feel refreshed. I didn't feel good at all.

We got a hotel room for the night. I laid back down and Holly went to inquire about a boat to Great Harbor. While she was gone, I broke out into a fever. I was burning up and drenched in sweat when she got back. After examining me, Holly said the wound was angry looking. It was infected. Must have been the duct tape, she told me. Off she went again in search of peroxide, Advil, and clean bandages. I hated that she had to take care of me. I couldn't recall ever being taken care of. Breeze didn't need the assistance of others. Breeze took care of himself.

She nursed me through the night. I got a peroxide bath every hour. When she ran out, she left to get more. She put a cool rag on my forehead. She had me double up on the antibiotics the hospital had given me. I was somewhat better by morning, but in no shape for a boat ride. We blew another two hundred bucks for another night in the hotel.

"I'm sorry to be a burden to you," I told Holly. "And I'm real sorry about your boat. Stick around long enough, you'll see how things go to Hell real fast. Story of my life."

"I'll hear none of that," she said. "I'll never be able to repay you for the boat repairs. At least I can help you back to good health."

"I bet I'll heal up faster laying on one of those beaches we found," I said. "Get us back to the boat. We're getting tan lines again."

Getting back to the boat did not improve my condition. The ride over made things worse. I couldn't shake the fever. I was weak, barely able to walk. Holly said I needed a hospital again. She was probably right, but I was stubborn. Hans was appalled at my appearance when we showed up at the marina. While I slept, he told Holly about a local woman who may be able to help.

I woke to the face of a very black Bahamian grandmother hovering over me.

"The sickness is deep in you," she said.

"Yea," I responded. "I'm down with the sickness."

"Aunt Sally will get the sickness out of you, boy," she said. "No sickness too vile for Aunt Sally."

"That's good news, Aunt Sally," I said. "Nice to meet you."

"You just hush now," she said. "Black salve and magic leaves for you now."

I tried to look around. I was on my boat. I couldn't see Holly. Things were fuzzy. A witch doctor named Aunt Sally was stuffing leaves in my mouth. She poured water in afterwards. I sputtered and choked.

"Swallow the leaves, boy," she said. "Powerful medicine."

I did as she instructed. She rolled me over like a sack of potatoes. I felt her applying glop to my wounds. It smelled like shit.

"You putting shit on my back, Aunt Sally?" I asked.

"Only smells like shit," she said. "Draws out the venom."

"I didn't get bit by a snake," I said.

"Don't give me no sass, boy," she said. "Try to sleep. Don't move."

She left the room. In spite of the horrible smell, I went back to sleep. My dreams were stupid vivid. Witch doctors with the faces of all the women from my past, danced around a fire.

Laura shook rattles at me. Joy made me drink from a painted gourd. Yolanda rubbed green leaves all over me. Andy ran feathers all over my body. Holly appeared holding a spear. She ran off the witchdoctors. She crouched by my side holding her spear. In the light of the fire I could see war paint on her face. She guarded me from the demons until I woke the next morning.

She was there when I opened my eyes. She wasn't wearing war paint or holding a spear.

"Welcome back," she said. "You must have been having a wild dream."

"Thanks," I said. "Thanks for looking over me."

# Nine

Aunt Sally administered to me daily. First she had Holly boil some water. She used an assortment of wash clothes and dish towels to clean off the old goop. Holly washed the wound with peroxide and then I got a new dose of goop. The smell ran Holly out of the room. It didn't seem to bother Aunt Sally.

My fever was gone. Apparently the wound was healing nicely. I could feel it tightening up. Eventually, I was declared cured of evil demons and such. It took a week for my bunk to stop smelling like shit. Holly washed my sheets three times. I was able to walk about freely.

"What did we pay Aunt Sally with?" I asked Holly. "Chickens and goats?"

"I haven't paid her a thing," she said. "She didn't ask."

"We have to give her something," I said. "I'm pretty sure she saved my life."

"A hospital would have saved you too," she said. "And you wouldn't have smelled so bad."

"I don't like hospitals," I said. "Bunch of sick people there. Never know what you might catch."

"I'll ask Hans how we settle up with Aunt Sally," she said.

While she was gone, I reacquainted myself with my boat. I'd been out of it for days, and hadn't left my bed. The interior was neat and clean, better than I usually kept it myself. There was a stack of books on the desk that Holly had borrowed from the marina's dayroom. I saw fresh fruits and vegetables on the galley counter. Flowers sat in a jar on the table. It was all very homey. Holly returned with word from Hans.

"He said she won't take your money, but if you suggest she donate it to the church, that might work."

"I don't like churches either," I said. "Nothing but sinners in them."

"You don't have to go to church," she said. "Just try to give the money to Aunt Sally. When she refuses, suggest the donation."

"Okay, let's go see her," I said. "Is it far?"

"Hans said to go out to the road and wait," she said. "Someone will come along and offer us a ride."

It worked just like Hans said. We stood by the road until the first car came along. It stopped. A friendly local asked where we were headed. Of course, he knew Aunt Sally. He dropped us at a little shack that was surrounded by herbs and flowers. Aunt Sally was bent over in the garden, holding up her dress with one hand and pulling weeds with the other.

"Well if it ain't Mr. Breeze," she said. "You must be feeling better."

"We came to thank you," I said. "And to give you this."

I held out five twenties towards her.

"Oh no, boy," she said. "I don't want your money."

"May I suggest that you give it to your church?" I said. "I have to repay you somehow, and I'm not up for yard work."

"I suppose that would be okay," she said.

I handed her the cash and watched her stuff into her ample bra.

"So what was that stuff you fixed me with?" I asked.

"Nature's remedies, son," she said. "Ain't no voodoo in it."

"My addled brain thought you were a witch doctor," I told her.

"Just old time island cures," she said. "I keep supplies handy. You never know when some boater will step on a stingray or get stung by a jellyfish. The local children sometimes eat the wrong berries or twist an ankle. I'm here for all of them."

"They're lucky to have you," I said. "I truly want to express my gratitude. Thanks so much."

"Haven't had a case like yours in a long time," she said. "Not since one-eyed Willie sliced up his neighbor with a machete. That'd be ten years or more by now."

"I hope it's a long time before you have another one," I said.

"Good Lord willing," she said. "Now run along. I got weeding to do."

No cars came along on our way back. By the time we reached the marina, I'd had enough walking for the day. I was still a little weak. I hadn't eaten much of anything for days. Holly fixed us a nice meal, and I was asleep soon after. All I did was rest and eat for the next week. Holly was getting fidgety. There wasn't a lot for a young person to do at the marina. She didn't much care for socializing with the other boaters. We both read books and took naps. At the end of the week she pressed me.

"We have to get out of here," she said. "I'm going stir crazy. I can read books on a beach someplace."

"I'm not ready to fight any battles," I said. "But I can get us to a beach. Let's roll."

"You sure you're going to be okay?" she asked. "Once we leave here, we won't be able to get help."

"I'm ready to go too," I said. "Just be gentle with me for a while."

The next day I sent Holly to get groceries. I went to see Hans. I thanked him profusely for everything. I wanted to do something to repay the staff. I was so grateful I wanted to repay the whole island. Hans suggested supplies for the school. I had no access to such things. He offered to send for them from off-island. I gave him five hundred bucks to help further the education of the local kids. He was excited to get it. It made me feel good to contribute. I paid up my own debt to the marina and told Hans we'd be moving on.

"You're welcome here anytime," he said.

It was nice to know I was back in his good graces.

We spent the next three weeks revisiting our previous anchorages. I continued to recover from my injuries. Slowly we worked our way down the Berry Island chain until we reached Chub Cay. There was a fancy marina there where we took on fuel and water. There was a defunct resort next door. The pool was clean even though no one was around. We spent the afternoon floating and lounging, pretending to be billionaires.

That evening we poured over charts while sipping cold beers. I pointed out some possible destinations for us to explore. My health was good. I felt much stronger. It was time to seek out new horizons, to change the angle of our sunsets, and to generally put some water under our keel. The ordeal was over. I told Holly it was time for another adventure.

"I've been down through the Exumas before," I said. "You really shouldn't miss it."

"How far is it?" she asked. "I'm ready to travel some."

"Nassau isn't far at all," I told her. "But I'd rather skip that circus. We can run down to Rose Island. The top of the Exumas is a short hop from there."

"Sounds good," she said.

"If everything goes smoothly," I said. "We can visit my old friend Captain Fred down in Georgetown."

I told Holly all about Captain Fred. He was very wealthy, but somehow we'd become friends. He lived on his seventy foot Hatteras, at anchor in Red Shanks. Every time I'd seen him or talked to him, I needed his help with something. It would be nice to visit without needing a favor. I owed him a lot. She was just anxious to get moving. She'd suffered my convalescence long enough. She hadn't signed on to be my nursemaid. I was determined to make it up to her. How much strength did it take to walk beaches, and watch sunsets? The only vigorous thing I needed to worry about, was making love to a much younger woman. Needless to say, I was excited to get moving too.

We steered away from the harbor entrance for Nassau, skirted around New Providence and made a course for Rose Island. We dodged numerous coral heads before we found a spot to anchor. We were removed from the chaos of casinos and resorts, but we could feel the frenetic energy that society emitted. We didn't stick around. The next morning we set off for Allens Cay. It was crowded when we arrived. We really hadn't anchored near other boats for a month. On the beach, iguanas pestered us, looking for a handout. It was beautiful, but we decided to move on.

Our next stop was Highbourne Cay. It was a short trip. The anchorage was less crowded, but dominated by a mega-yacht. We spent one night at anchor, then relocated to the Highbourne Cay Marina. We had a nice, but expensive meal at the restaurant there. Still searching for more seclusion, we traveled a bit further south to Normans Cay. We anchored south of Galleon Point in six feet of water with good protection. We spent a few days exploring North Harbour and Normans Pond by dinghy.

Warderick Wells was our next port of call. We took a mooring ball just off the Exuma Cays Land and Sea Park. Holly wanted to dive and bring up some lobsters, but it was forbidden within park boundaries. Instead we visited the park headquarters and pick up a snorkeling map for the cays and reefs within the park. We also got a hiking map that detailed the many trails on the island. We spent a week trying to do and see everything that the park had to offer. Other boats came and went. It was a popular stop, but it never felt crowded.

A perfect weather window presented itself so we decided to tear ourselves away. We spent another week moving about several anchorages at Staniel Cay. It was a bustling little settlement with a lot to offer. The surrounding waters were some of the most spectacular that we'd seen yet. The people were cheery. The shops were good. There was a variety of services available. Everything we could want or need was within easy walking distance. We stocked up on some delicious homemade bread. We wandered the streets, admiring the pastel colored buildings. I felt no ill-effects from the exercise or the long days without rest. I was almost back in fighting shape. I tested that with an athletic roll in the hay. No damage was done. We hadn't made love since I got hurt, so it was good to be back in the saddle again. Unfortunately, we didn't equal that passion of our tryst on Holly's sailboat. Don't get me wrong, it was great, but that day out on the open ocean with her had been unforgettable.

We sat and talked as the sun went down.

"I think I liked the Berry's better," she said. "There so many boats here, so many people."

"It will thin out south of here," I said. "Most of these boats are heading north for the summer. We seem to be swimming against the tide."

"Aren't we always?" she laughed.

"Georgetown gets crowded, but it's not so bad in the summer time," I said. "Half of them go back to the states. The other half heads further south to hide from hurricanes."

"Should we be worried about hurricanes?" she asked.

"Georgetown is as good a place as any to ride one out," I said. "You can get internet there. At least will know if one's coming."

"I don't get you sometimes," she said.

"What's not to get?" I asked.

"You like, study and plan everything when we're traveling," she said. "You are a great captain, down to the last detail, but with the really important stuff, you just wing it. Going to capture a bad guy; you'll figure something out. Hurricane; we don't need a plan."

"That's funny," I said. "The truth is I wing it when I don't know what to do. You can only plan so much. The rest comes down to luck and a cool head."

"That storm that wrecked my boat was a serious case of bad luck," she said.

"We survived," I said. "Shit went all to hell but we kept our cool. We adapted. We overcame."

"You're trying to say it could have been worse," she said.

"Damn straight it could have been worse," I said. "Most people would have died out there, or abandoned ship and hoped for a rescue."

"I didn't panic," she said. "I was afraid, but I didn't let it get to me. I'm proud of how I handled it, but you, you were amazing. I've never seen anyone handle pressure like you did."

"I think maybe I've had too much experience in pressure situations," I said. "One of these days it might catch up to me."

"Not likely," she said. "You got sliced open like a fish being fileted. Now you're good as new."

"I just lost my appetite for fish," I said.

"You're going to get mighty hungry then," she laughed.

Before heading south, we took a trip to Big Majors to see the pigs. The freckled fatties swam right out to us to beg. Holly fed them carrots and almost lost a finger in the process. The next morning we left for Great Guana Cay, and the Black Point Settlement. We entered a bight formed by Dotham Point to the north, and Black Point to the south. We found good holding northeast of the government dock in seven feet of water. There were a bunch of boats in the neighborhood. Holly gave me a "what the fuck" look as we settled in on anchor. I shrugged and got us each a beer. We stayed long enough to take advantage of the free water, and the best laundromat in the islands. We took our book collection and swapped them out for new reads at Lorraine's Café.

We continued south to Little Farmers Cay. There were only two other boats. Little beaches were spread about the coves and cays. The water was deep, crystal blue. It was gorgeous. We spent a week and never sat on the same beach twice. We were alone for a few days, before more boats came in. There were never more than four at a time, and they stayed well-spaced. It was just enough company for us to keep our clothes on.

Finally, we decided to just go ahead and make the run down to Georgetown. I was certain that the out islands south of there would be more deserted. We both longed for an empty beach. Our favorite times were when we were completely alone together. We'd both deepened our aversion to being around other people. We never fit in, even with seasoned cruisers. They talked about politics, sports scores, and silly things they saw on Facebook. I hadn't seen a ballgame of any kind in five years. I was vaguely aware of who the president was. I didn't own a cell phone, let alone a computer. I didn't watch TV or read newspapers. My world revolved around the weather and the tides. I lived for sunsets and the pull of a fish on my line. I had absolutely nothing in common with those people.

Elizabeth Harbor in Georgetown was thankfully not very crowded. By that, I mean there was only forty or fifty boats. During the winter months, it fills with hundreds of vessels. We were able to anchor within sight of *Incognito,* Captain Fred's boat. It would be a long dinghy ride to the town docks, but it afforded a certain amount of privacy. Fred's dinghy was not tied to his boat, so we went off to search for him. He never went far. We located him on the beach at the Redshanks Yacht and Tennis Club. There were no tennis courts to be found. He was commanding an audience of cruisers, telling tales as usual. His unlit cigar was chewed to a nub.

"By God it's the dope smuggling pirate from Florida come to pay us a visit," he said. "And who is this interesting creature by your side?"

"Good to see you too, Fred," I said. "This is Holly. She's a bit of a hippie but she's a hell of a sailor."

Holly jabbed me on the arm and introduced herself.

"What sort of trouble have you gotten yourself into this time?" he asked. "The man never comes to see me without needing a favor."

"I've broken that streak," I said. "We've come a very long way just to visit with you. We don't need anything from you at all."

"I'm deeply touched," he said. "Been a long time coming."

"I realize that," I said. "I've been trying to make amends lately. I owe you."

"Bringing me pretty young ladies is repayment enough," he said. "You'll need to stay long enough to tell me how you do it. Then we'll be even."

"We'll hang out a little bit," I said. "But we're thinking about continuing south."

"Where'd you come from this time?" he asked.

"Florida, by way of Grand Cayman," I said. "Berry Islands for a while."

"Still filled with wanderlust," he said. "Dragging this poor girl all over the seven seas."

"She's got it worse than I do," I said. "She's doing the dragging. I'm just happy to be along for the ride."

"Maybe you've finally met your match then, Breeze," he said. "Never thought I'd see the day."

"We're just having a good time, island hopping," I said. "Holly's boat is down in Marathon. We'll have to get back sooner or later."

"Dinner on my boat tomorrow evening," he said. "Bring nothing but your appetites. I've had some fine beef flown in from the mainland."

"We've been eating fish and lobster for two months," said Holly.

"Yea, beef sounds really good," I said. "Thanks captain."

We let him return to his story telling and made our way back to *Leap of Faith*. It was about time to give the boat some attention. We'd traveled far enough to warrant an oil change and other necessary maintenance items.

"He seems like a pretty cool guy," said Holly.

"He is," I said. "And he's got a billion dollars in the bank. He also has a very colorful past. He's a real good person to know."

"A couple months ago we were hanging out with One-legged Beth and Diver Dan," she said. "Now we're having dinner with a billionaire."

"I don't know what Fred sees in me," I said. "But he's gotten me out of some serious jams."

"From bums to billionaires, Breeze," she said. "You're really something."

"People are people," I said. "There's a damn few good ones. When you find them, you stick with them regardless of their bank account."

# Ten

I put on my best shirt again. Holly put on her wrinkly sundress. Neither one of us wore shoes. When we boarded Fred's boat, he took Holly's hand and kissed it. She blushed. He served us filet mignon. It was seared perfectly on the outside. It was blood red on the inside. It had the texture of butter and it tasted like the food of the Gods. I declined the asparagus. Fred told me it would put hair on my chest. I told him that it made my pee smell funny.

We laughed and joked throughout the meal. Fred was an old, balding, stubby guy, but he was charming. He loosened Holly up in no time. They shared animated stories. He made her comfortable. He joked that he was the better catch. Maybe she should stay there with him. She joked that she just might. After dinner he gave us each a snifter of brandy and a fine cigar. To my surprise, Holly lit hers up.

We sat together in a haze of smoke, full bellies, and good booze. Everyone was smiling. We were all loose and happy. That's when he hit me with it.

"The tables have turned, my young friend," he said to me. "I have a favor to ask of you."

"Shoot, Fred," I said. "Anything I can do to help. What is it?"

"It's my daughter," he began. "Long story that I'll try to make short."

Before leaving Florida, Fred had been docked in Punta Gorda. His youngest daughter, the wayward one, had come to stay on his boat. Just down the dock lived a squirrely character named Theren. The two of them started hanging out. Fred had him investigated. He didn't like what he learned. He moved his boat down to the Fort Myers City Yacht Basin. Theren followed soon after. Fred had confronted his daughter's suitor, forbidding him to contact her.

"What was wrong with the guy?" I asked.

"He was married for one thing," said Fred. "But he was also a mooching loser. He was living on some bogus workmen's comp claim. Supposedly had a bad back. I saw him working on his boat, carrying heavy shit, stuff like that. He should have been working a job, not working my daughter."

"So where do I come in?" I asked.

"As soon as I left Florida," he said. "She moved onto his puny ass boat. They're shacked up together. I won't stand for it."

"What is it that you want me to do, Fred?" I asked.

"I want you to take her away from him, and get her here to me," he said. "I can hire any number of thugs to deal with him, but I need someone I can trust to take care of my daughter."

"What if she doesn't want to leave?" I asked.

"I don't care if you have to hog-tie her," he said. "Just get her away from him. Get her on a plane to Georgetown. I'll deal with the fallout when she arrives."

"He's a little guy, you said?" I asked.

"He's a pussy, Breeze," he answered. "I don't see how it would be dangerous for you. My daughter is easily led by authority. Just be firm with her. I'll doubt she'll be a problem either."

"Where are they now?" I asked.

"Last known location was the Fort Myers Yacht Basin," he said. "He wasn't much of a sailor. He's probably still there."

"Okay, I'll need some specifics about him and his boat in case he's moved," I said.

Fred tossed a thick file on the table.

"Everything I know is in that file," he said.

"Wait a minute," said Holly. "I thought you were out of this line of work."

I explained to Fred how my last job with Tom Melendez had gone awry. I told him how badly I'd been hurt afterwards, and that I was just now on the mend. We kicked it back and forth, before finally deferring to Holly. We decided that if she was dead set against it, that I wouldn't take the job. She promised to think it over. We said goodnight and left.

Back on board my boat, Holly paced the deck.

"I know you want to do this," she said.

"I won't argue my case too hard," I said. "I appreciate where you're coming from. It's just that I owe Captain Fred so much. Without him, I'd certainly be in jail right now. I might even be dead, who knows?"

"Christ, Breeze," she said. "You make it hard for me to say no."

"If you weren't in the picture," I said. "There'd be no question. But you are, so you have a say."

"I can't be the reason you let him down," she said. "Go ahead and do it."

"Will you come with me?" I asked.

"I will, but I'm real wary about this," she said.

"You've got time to think it over," I said. "You're boat should be ready soon. If we get to Florida and you want to bail, just say the word."

"Fair enough," she said. "But I'll stick it out. We're sort of partners now, you know."

It was settled. Holly and Breeze had a mission.

We filled in the details with Fred the next morning. He offered an unlimited expense account, giving me one of his credit cards. He offered no payment for completion of the job. I was a friend repaying all the favors he'd done for me.

"Just get her here to me in one piece, Breeze," he said. "I'll take it from there."

We did not take our time on the trip back. We ran long days when the weather was right, skipping over many of the anchorages we'd visited on the way down. We did not run at night until we left Chub Cay to cross the banks. We hunkered down behind Gun Cay while the wind blew. We made a break for it as soon as the wind calmed. We motored day and night straight for Marathon, fighting against the Gulf Stream part of the way.

Upon arrival in Boot Key Harbor, we slept for a few hours, but Holly was anxious to see her boat. Howie stopped us before we could get into the boatyard.

"No, no, no," he said, waving his arms at us. "No one gets in until she's finished."

"Oh come on, Howie," pled Holly. "I'm dying to see her."

"We'll have a proper unveiling at the proper time," he said.

"What's the holdup?" she asked.

"A few small details to finish, and one big one," he answered.

"What's the big one?" she asked.

"The boat didn't have no name on it when it came in," he said. "Don't know what name to put on it now. I got the best letter man in the Keys waiting for a name."

"Yea, Holly," I said. "You never have said what the name was."

"I never decided," she said. "Until just recently. I just didn't have the depth of experience to know what to name it."

"What's it gonna be?" Howie asked.

"*Another Adventure*," said Holly.

"No shit," I said.

"Why?" she asked. "What's the matter with *Another Adventure*?"

"Nothing," I said. "It's a great name."

"Come on, Breeze," she said. "What's the matter?"

"You remember the girl that died in Miami?" I asked.

"You told me about her," she said. "Joy, wasn't it?"

"Yes, Joy," I said. "That was the name of her boat. *Another Adventure.*"

"Unfortunate coincidence," she said. "I don't know what to say. Is it going to be a problem for you?"

"It's not my boat," I said. "Won't be a problem. Fond memories. Bad ones too, but it will be fine. It's a perfect name for you."

"Another Adventure it is," said Howie. "Come back in a week or two. You're going to love it."

We topped off on fuel and headed north the very next day. It sure was nice having another competent captain on board. All those times that I'd made the trip up the west coast of Florida, I'd always had to stop off at various points along the way. With Holly and myself sharing time at the wheel, we could just keep on motoring through the night. We didn't even have to worry too much about snagging crab pots. She was an excellent diver. If we caught one, she could just go over the side and free it. We managed to skip over the anchorages at Little Shark, Marco and Fort Myers Beach. Instead, we cruised right on up the Caloosahatchee River. We dropped the hook near a small island, just out from the City of Fort Myers Yacht Basin. That's where this Theren character would be found.

His boat was a piece junk. It wasn't dirty or

unkempt, it was just a poor quality vessel, built by some off-brand company I'd never heard of. According to the information supplied by Captain Fred, he'd bought it for four thousand dollars. The owner was in financial trouble, and had been offered half that. The sale was about to go through when Theren stumbled in and doubled the offer. He didn't sound like the sharpest tack.

We waited for a neighbor to take their dinghy to shore. We simply followed them to determine where he got access to land. We tied up and walked into the marina. We found the boat, but no one was aboard. The hatches were open and it wasn't locked. They couldn't be gone long.

"So what's the plan when they show up?" asked Holly.

"Fred said the guy is a punk," I replied. "I say we just rush onto the boat, separate the girl, and split."

"That's it?" she asked. "No details?"

"We just hop aboard," I said. "I'll hold off the boyfriend. You lead her away and I'll follow. We'll have a car waiting."

"Sounds simple enough," she said. "What are the chances of it being that easy?"

"Pretty good, I think," I said. "What's he going to do? Fly into a rage and attack us? If so I'll deal with it. You worry about Fred's daughter."

We called Enterprise Car Rentals. Using Fred's credit card, we arranged for a car and a pick-up at the marina. We browsed flights to Georgetown with Holly's phone. There were no direct flights from Fort Myers. Everything went through Fort Lauderdale. We couldn't put her on a flight that changed planes. It would be too easy for her to escape before making it to her father. Fred would be waiting at the airport on Great Exuma. We'd have to drive her to Lauderdale, put her on the plane, and make sure she stayed on it. It might also throw off her boyfriend if he tried to pursue us.

We saw them in the marina parking lot. They were getting out of the car, carrying groceries. We watched them walk down to the docks and disappear.

"You ready?" I asked Holly.

"I guess," she said. "This is what we came for."

We walked after them. They were just loading the last of their bags onboard when we reached their boat. Holly and I looked at each other and nodded. We both jumped aboard. Fred's daughter was inside. Theren dashed inside too. I went in first and informed them that the girl was leaving with us. Holly followed and took her by the arm.

"What the hell is going on?" screamed Theren.

He was indeed a little guy. He stood about five foot, four inches tall. He wasn't rail thin, but he wasn't muscular either. He had fear in his eyes.

"Look," I said. "I don't know you, so I don't want to have to hurt you. We are taking her to see her father. She can come peacefully with everyone cooperating, or we can play it rough."

He looked down at the floor and didn't reply.

Fred's daughter made a small effort to pull away from Holly, who tightened her grip. The spoiled girl-child of a billionaire was no match for Holly. She looked down at the floor too.

"Take her outside," I said to Holly.

I stepped in front of the companionway after they left to block Theren. When I turned to face him, he was holding a small gun. It was a tiny thing. It looked like something a woman would carry in her purse. He was unsteady.

"You're not taking her," he said. "Bring her back right now."

"I told you we didn't want any violence," I said. "Now it's going to have to get ugly, unless you put that away."

He waved the little gun at me and yelled for me to get out of his way. He stepped too close. I grabbed his wrist, twisted it, and took the gun with my other hand. He was disarmed in about a second. For good measure, I smacked him in the face with it. He went down and I went after Holly.

The two girls were a hundred yards ahead of me. I caught up and we all walked to the parking lot like nothing was out of the ordinary. Fred's daughter just walked with her head down, saying nothing. Holly sat in the back seat with her and I drove. We traveled for an hour before she spoke.

"I'll never get away from my father," she said. "It's my life, but he won't let me live it."

"He sending you an allowance?" I asked. "Or are you paying your own way?"

"He sends money," she said.

"Well there you have it," I said. "His money, his choice. When you pay your own way you can make your own way."

"You wouldn't understand," she said.

"Of course I wouldn't," I said. "I don't have a billionaire daddy to take care of me."

"He's probably paying you to do this," she said. "Or you wouldn't do it. That's what he does. He buys people."

"If you must know," I said. "I'm doing this as a favor for my good friend. He's covering expenses only, like this car, and your plane ticket."

"I'll pay you to take me back," she said. "Just turn around and let me go. No questions asked. I have some money."

"Breeze doesn't need your money, honey," said Holly. "Just sit back and enjoy the ride. Get comfortable."

The girl went silent and we drove on. Holly reserved a one-way flight to Georgetown. Occasionally, the girl would sigh loudly and look at us for a reaction. We ignored her. We showed her no pity. I knew very little about her, but Fred had always referred to her as the "Wayward One," whenever he mentioned her. I suspect she'd been a problem child. I told myself I was doing the right thing. Fred would straighten her out. She'd become a happier person in the long run. I trusted Fred. There was nothing his daughter could say that would make me believe he was a monster, or even a bad parent.

We finally pulled into the airport late in the afternoon. As soon as we got out of the car, our prisoner took off running. It was a sorry sight. She was far from athletic. Holly and I took off after her. We caught up to her quickly. She started to scream.

"Help me, help me!" she yelled. "I'm being kidnapped."

I put my hand over her mouth and twisted her ear. She stopped screaming, but she tried to stomp my foot. A passerby asked if everything was all right.

"She needs her medication," I said. "We need to get her inside and get some pills in her."

The stranger continued walking with a distrusting look. I was afraid they might go to a cop or security guard. I put my prisoner's arm behind her back caused her a little pain. She stopped struggling.

"If you behave, this will all go smoothly and painlessly," I told her. "If not, I'll put you in the trunk of the car for a few hours, while you calm down."

"Please let me go," she said. "I'll stop fighting, but please just let me go."

"I don't know what you're so afraid of," I said. "You'll be living on a luxury yacht in the Bahamas. What's not to like?"

"I won't be free," she said.

I had no snappy comeback for that. I understood freedom. It was the most precious thing in life to me. My boat, the sea, and my freedom were what made life worth living. I'd gone through great pains, and a whole lot of money, in order to preserve my freedom. Still, I couldn't let her guilt me into not fulfilling my mission. I simply couldn't free her. I'd let my last prisoner, Tom Melendez, go free. That had been the right thing to do. This time, I owed a debt to this girl's father. He was my friend. She was not. She was going to the Bahamas, no matter what.

"Come on," I told her, pulling her arm. "You've got a plane to catch."

She followed without resistance.

When we got to the check-in counter, we discovered that the flight we'd reserved changed planes in Nassau. That wouldn't do. Our captive would have another chance to get away. The customer service representative went over all our options with us. There was simply no direct flight into Georgetown available. We had no choice but to purchase three tickets. We were going to Nassau with her. I hated the idea, but couldn't figure out a better solution.

While we waited for the flight, we went to the Enterprise booth to extend the rental on the car. Then I remembered that *Leap of Faith* was anchored unattended in the river at Fort Myers. Events were not unfolding as smoothly as I hoped. I was pretty good at adapting to changing circumstances. Holly was not. She was irritated and stressed. Airports are busy places with too many people and too much noise. The girl we were transporting could have caused us trouble at any moment. We were hungry and tired.

"This sucks, Breeze," said Holly.

"I agree," I said. "But it will all be over soon. We make a quick turnaround in Nassau and go back home."

"I don't have a home," she said. "My boat is still on the hard. I don't know where home is even when it's in the water."

"I guess Pelican Bay is as close to home as I've ever gotten," I said. "But the Berry Islands sure were nice."

"What is it with you and Pelican Bay?" she asked. "It's nice and all, but there are so many other nice places."

"It's where I go to mend my soul," I said. "It's saved me several times. I feel at peace there. When things go to hell, I go back there and heal."

"I thought I needed a place like that," she said. "But now, I think I just want to stay on the move. I can't wait to get my boat back."

"Soon enough," I said.

We finally boarded the plane. The flight was short but crowded. All of the other passengers were on a vacation and excited about the fun to come. The three of us were depressed. We trudged across the tarmac in Nassau. Fred's daughter dreaded her reunion. We dreaded our flight back. We had called Fred from Lauderdale and he was waiting when we landed. He carried an overnight bag, which he offered to his daughter. He suggested she freshen up before they leave for Georgetown. I thought it was thoughtful of him. He used a head motion to get Holly to stand guard outside the ladies room. Once they were gone, he held out his hand to me.

"I knew I could trust you," he said. "Thanks an awful damn lot, my friend."

"Glad to help," I said. "I still probably owe you, but at least I've begun to pay my debt."

"All debts are hereby forgiven," he said. "Not that I ever expected to be repaid. Did you have any trouble?"

"Her punk-ass boyfriend pulled a little popgun on me," I said. "Then she tried to run and raise a fuss in Lauderdale. Wasn't nearly as smooth as I'd hoped."

"Sorry about that," he said. "I never dreamed you'd have trouble. I'd have sent some muscle along if I thought it was dangerous."

"I would have refused," I said. "Holly and I took care of it."

"What is your plan with that one?" he asked. "You never seem to hold on for long."

"I'd like to hold on this time," I said, honestly. "But I doubt she'll see it that way."

"The more free the spirit, the harder it is to hold," he said. "No doubt several women have said the same about you."

"No doubt," I said. "You're a wise man, Fred."

"I didn't get this rich being a dumbass," he said.

"Help your daughter make a life for herself," I said. "I'm sure you know what you're doing. Just give her a path to freedom, eventually."

"Boat bum wisdom for the wise man," he said. "I hear you, Breeze. I only want what's best for her."

"You two will work it out," I said. "I have faith in you."

The girls returned. Fred thanked me again. I bought return tickets for Holly and myself, and gave Fred his credit card back. He took his daughter gently by the arm and left the airport. By the time we got back to Lauderdale we were too tired to drive. We got a hotel room and crashed for the night. No love was made.

We scarfed down our free continental breakfast in the morning before starting our drive.

"That deal was not a lot of fun, Breeze," said Holly. "I don't think I'm cut out for this stuff."

"I'm real sorry," I said. "I only did it because it was Captain Fred. I'm done now."

"I'm done regardless," she said. "If you take another job, it will be without me."

"I understand," I said. "But I don't intend to look for trouble anytime soon."

"Good," she said. "Let's get back and start having fun again."

We made the long drive from Fort Lauderdale to Fort Myers. Holly called Enterprise so they could pick up the car. We walked down to the dinghy dock, keeping an eye out for that weasel Theren. We didn't see him. As soon as we cleared the sea wall, I looked for *Miss Leap*. Something wasn't right. She wasn't sitting in the water properly. I gave the little outboard all it had and pointed it out to Holly. As we got closer, we could see that she was listing badly. My heart sunk. I panicked.

I'd kept my cool when men fired bullets all through my boat. I didn't panic when a large man tried to beat me to death. I'd been afraid a few times, but I'd never panicked until that day. My boat was my entire world. I had nothing without her. She'd gotten me through flood and hellfire. Now she was sinking. She was sinking in a filthy river full of mud and pollutants. Her potential graveyard was surrounded by tall buildings and asphalt.

In my panic, I scrambled aboard without securing the dinghy. Holly was still aboard. She had enough sense to restart the motor and bring the little boat back. I noticed that the discharge from the secondary bilge pump was spitting out water. The outlet for the main pump was not. I ran to the well that housed the main pump. Water was up to the flooring. I reached down through the muddy water and felt around. The float was up, but the pump did not run. I found the wires. They'd been cut. The bare ends were under water. The fuse was certainly blown as well. *Stop the water, Breeze.*

I'd almost sunk her once before. The culprit was the hose coming from the raw water intake for the engine. I ran to that hatch. The clamps had been loosed and the hose separated from the thru-hull. I closed the shutoff and water stopped pouring in.

I opened the main floor hatch in the salon. Water had reached the bottom of the batteries, but they weren't floating. Most of the engine was still above water, but the transmission was not. Some of the lower wiring was also underwater. It would have to be replaced.

"What do you want me to do?" asked Holly.

"Get a bucket from the bridge," I yelled.

I grabbed a hand pump. Together, we filled the bucket and dumped it overboard about a thousand times. It took hours to make any headway at all. Eventually, I could get to the cut wires in order to splice them together. I didn't have time to do it properly, I just trimmed back the plastic coating and twisted them together. I found a replacement fuse and the pump sprang to life.

We both ran to the side of the boat to watch the twin streams of water pour out. Both pumps were up and running. *Leap of Faith* would not go down that day. We hugged, ignoring our mud and sweat covered bodies. There was mud and water everywhere inside the boat. She was a disaster.

"God, where do we start?" asked Holly.

"We start with a beer," I said. "Then I'll need to drain the transmission."

"You think it was Theren?" she asked.

"No doubt about it," I answered.

"What are you going to do?"

"Hunt him and kill him," I said.

"You don't mean that," she said.

"Okay, so I won't kill him," I said. "But he'll pay."

"Another mission," she said. "It hasn't even been a day."

She was right. I'd basically promised no more missions that very morning. Now, I wanted to track the bastard to the ends of the earth and get my revenge. I wanted to sink his boat. I'd hold his head and make him watch it go down. I'd rip off his head and shit down his throat afterwards. Was it worth losing Holly?

"You need to cool down and think about this," she said. "We've got a lot of work to do before you can chase down anybody."

"You're right," I said. "I need to think it over. I'll consider letting it go. You and I can just go about our life together, maybe."

"Will you resent me if I don't want you to go after him?" she asked.

"It's a possibility," I said. "Maybe even probable."

"Maybe we should sleep on it," she said.

"Good idea," I said. "But first I've got to change the oil in the tranny."

"Can I help?" she asked.

"Not enough room," I said. "Keep me in beers. That'll be a big help."

The bilge had a thin coating of mud on everything. It made working in the tight confines even more miserable than usual. The old oil came out milky white, which meant it had water in it. I refilled it with new fluid, and drained it again. It took four times before the oil was clean. I decided to change the engine oil too, just in case. It came out showing no signs of water. That was a good sign. The engine started normally. I put her in and out of gear. The transmission seemed to work fine.

As the engine warmed up, I noticed the tachometer was not working. I traced the wires and discovered that the tach wire had been fully submerged. One of the connections had shorted out. More problems would arise as we tried out all systems. I didn't have enough wire or connectors to fix it all. Once I was satisfied that the engine and transmission were operational, I gave up for the day.

I was still seething about Theren. Holly was deep in thought. She started to speak, but I shushed her.

"We're going to sleep on it," I said. "No sense in arguing tonight."

"Sensible people don't argue when they're covered in mud and smell like river bottom," she said.

We took deck showers, naked. We put our muddy clothes in a bucket of fresh water to soak. Most people would have just thrown them away, but neither of us owned clothes to spare. She shivered as I hosed off her back. There was a stubborn spot of mud on her ass that I had to rub off with my hand. She didn't believe my story, but let me do my thing. I gave her the hose and she cleaned up my backside as well. Once we introduced soap to the equation, things got all slippery and fun. I forgot about killing Theren for a few minutes.

The water level inside the boat had not reached the furniture or the bedsheets, but everything felt damp. Between the discomfort and my racing thoughts, I couldn't sleep. When I did doze off, I saw myself holding Theren's severed head, while his boat burned to the waterline. It was an ugly picture that stuck with me when I awoke.

Holly said she hadn't slept well either. She tried to find something for breakfast, but little was to be had. The boat smelled like muck. We realized the refrigerator wasn't working. It was a bad start to the day. I made coffee and tried to clear my head.

"That little fucker did a number on us, Breeze," said Holly.

"I cut his fool head off in my dreams," I told her. "Burned his crappy boat too."

"We've got to go get him," she said.

"We?" I asked. "Change of heart overnight?"

"I was part of this," she said. "I went along willingly. Now I'm seeing it through."

"You don't have to do this," I said. "You're boat is probably done by now, or almost. I can take you to Marathon first, then go after him myself."

"You'll give him too much of a head start," she said. "You know that."

"We can forget it then," I said. "Maybe I can hire Howie's guys to clean up this mess. Fix whatever else is wrong."

"You'll do no such thing," she said. "You find people. Where do you think he'd run to?"

"First we check his slip," I said. "Maybe he's dumb enough to still be around. If he's gone we'll ask his neighbors if he mentioned where he was going."

"Then what?" she said. "What if we get nothing?"

"As far as I know," I said. "He's never been anywhere but here and Punta Gorda. Fred's dossier says he bought the boat at Laishley Marina, then followed Fred here. He was surprised he made it that far."

"So maybe he went back there?" she asked.

"Seems logical," I said. "Good place to start."

"We need food and cleaning supplies," she said.

"Let's go down to Fort Myers Beach," I said. "We'll shake out the problems with the boat on the way. We can get groceries in the dinghy. There's a NAPA just across the bridge."

"Fire this tub up, captain," she said. "We've got a mission."

"First we go to the marina," I said. "Ask around."

His boat was gone. There were no neighbors about. The dock master didn't even know he was gone. There was no reason to stick around. He had run.

On the way down the river, we noted everything that didn't work. The gauges on the bridge flickered on and off. A few of the lights wouldn't come on. Overall though, it wasn't as bad as it could have been. The worst thing was the smell from the muddy bilge. I'd changed the fuse on the fridge and it came on.

We took a mooring ball and got right to work. I loaded a cart with food while Holly picked out the cleaning supplies. Back on board we dumped Simple Green into the bilge and let it soak. I chased down bad wire connections and repaired them. I redid the bilge pump wiring completely. We pumped the cleaner and the dirty water overboard. The water was so nasty in the harbor these days, no one noticed. It was a damn shame. Fort Myers Beach used to have nice blue water. Now it was a thick brown goo that reeked of chemicals and dead organisms.

We added more Simple Green and scrubbed. We rinsed it with fresh water until the tanks ran dry. Then I had to ferry jugs back and forth to refill the water tanks. It took hours and wore me out. I took a break and used Holly's phone to call Laishley Park Marina. Rusty answered. I asked him about my old pal Theren.

"He's on a mooring ball," said Rusty. "Just got here. We didn't have a slip available for him. Don't figure one will open up soon."

"So no slip available for me either?" I asked.

"Sorry, Breeze," he said. "We're full up."

"No problem," I said. "Don't mention I was asking about him, if you don't mind."

"I never talk to the dude," he said. "Strange little fellow."

"Maybe I'll see you," I said. "Thinking about coming up and anchoring off Gilchrest."

"Cross-eyed John is still over there," he said. "Just saying."

"Okay, thanks," I said. "Have a good one."

Theren was in Punta Gorda. He was on a mooring ball in the Peace River. We had some groceries, and a good start on cleaning up. He wasn't likely to leave there anytime soon. He'd just arrived, after all. I had the impression that traveling wasn't his favorite thing to do. He'd only moved that boat once before now. He was a sitting duck. I only needed to figure out what I was going to do to him.

We took advantage of the real showers provided with our mooring fee. We got a pizza at the Upper Deck. We stayed to listen to music and drink beers when the pizza was gone.

"What do you want to do with him?" asked Holly.

"Sink his boat," I said. "Wreck it or burn it or something."

"Is that going to be enough for you?" she asked.

"I don't need to hurt him," I said. "He doesn't understand where I'm coming from. I came in, stole his girlfriend away. He hates me. He can't comprehend that I was doing it for my friend. He doesn't know that I owed Fred a favor. He just sees me as the bad guy. I'm surprised he had the balls to sabotage my boat. Good on him, I guess. Now I return the favor."

"I don't want him hurt either," she said. "He seems like an innocent bystander in this."

"He lost his innocence when he tried to sink my boat," I said. "He needs to see that he can't get away with that. Fred has his reasons to dislike the guy. They're probably valid."

"So, we sink his boat, then this will be over, right?" she said. "We go back to fun in the sun."

"Every time I make a promise," I said. "Something happens to make me break it. Something out of my control. I want fun in the sun, Holly, believe me, but maybe I should refrain from making any promises."

"Shit doesn't always work out?" she prodded.

"Oh it works out," I said. "Just not always the way you wished it did."

"Truth," she said.

Back on the boat, we sat in silence on the aft deck. We watched the traffic on the bridge, the anchor lights blinking on, and the steady flow of the tide. I was trying to think things through. Holly didn't interrupt. She was deep in her own thoughts.

All of my episodes with women ended up with me being alone. They were not the same though. My wife, Laura, had died. Andi had been a special person, but I'd been stuck in my grief and full of angst. I didn't love her back like she deserved. I let her go without a fight. With Yolanda, I had been the strong one. I'd saved her life. I'd guided her to a new one. Even though I was alone at the end, I felt good about it. I'd been selfless that time. I'd gone along with Joy's antics because I didn't want to lose her. I'd given up control. It ended with her death. I'd never truly known Taylor. I was infatuated with her hotness. She screwed me so well in bed, that I was blind to how she'd screwed me in life. Now here I was, sitting on my boat with Holly. I'd felt that my hold on her was tenuous, but she'd stayed when offered the chance to leave. Our relationship was as honest and true as when I was married, but something wasn't there. We were intimate as friends, but when it came to love, we were both holding back.

Theren was a gnat that bothered me. I wanted to swat his ass and be done with it. I wondered what would happen after it was done. What would happen with Holly and me? I knew that her boat was calling her. I completely understood. I could not stand between her and her boat. I wouldn't let her stand between me and mine. That's where it would end. I knew it at that moment.

# Eleven

Charlotte Harbor is a beautiful bay that runs from the Gulf of Mexico at Boca Grande Pass, up to Punta Gorda and Port Charlotte at its northern end. It's fed by the Myakka and Peace Rivers. The mooring field where we could find our quarry was in the Peace River, just beyond two bridges that cross it. There is very little development on Charlotte Harbor. It makes for a scenic cruise. Only two tall buildings break the mangrove horizon. They mark the entrance to Burnt Store Marina on the east wall of the harbor. Punta Gorda means Fat Point in Spanish. As you approach the town, you veer out around the point in order to avoid shallow water.

## Bahama Breeze

There are a few condominium complexes on the banks there. The first major landmark is Fishermen's Village. There's a marina there, but it also includes villas, shops and restaurants. The entrance channel is well marked. We cut in from the center of the harbor just past those markers and anchored a few hundred yards outside the marina. I wanted to be out of sight from the mooring field. If I couldn't see Theren's boat, he couldn't see mine. There were a scattering of other vessels anchored a little further upriver, off Gilchrest Park. Cross-eyed John's was one of them. He'd painted his topsides neon green. It was hard to miss.

John and I had a long history. Unfortunately, his personal story was a sad one. He was a hopeless alcoholic. When he was drinking, he made really poor decisions. He was drinking most of the time, so he was always doing stupid shit. I'd tried to help him out from time to time without getting too involved in his life. We only crossed paths occasionally. It seemed like he'd made a permanent residence for himself in Punta Gorda lately.

It wasn't long before he saw my boat and made his way over to say hello. His dinghy was filthy and full of junk. He wore badly worn shorts and no shirt or shoes. He looked thinner than when I'd seen him last.

"What ya doing back here, Breeze?" he asked. "I thought you were off in the islands someplace."

"I was, for a while," I said. "Something came up. I've got a little business to attend to here."

"What happened to that redhead you left here with?" he asked.

"Old news," I said. "Let me introduce you to Holly."

They shook hands in greeting after John climbed aboard.

"I dig your hair," he said to Holly.

"Thanks," she said. "Can I get you something to drink?"

John turned to me. I could see sadness in his eyes. He looked worn down.

"I could really use a meal," he said. "I'm sorry to impose on you, but I'm starving out here."

"How bad is the drinking?" I asked.

"It got real bad, Breeze," he said. "But I'm sober right now. I've got no money for booze. Hell, I ain't go not money for food."

"What are you going to do, John?" I asked him.

"I don't know, man," he admitted. "The bums in the park exclude me from whatever charity they get. I try panhandling on the other side of the river sometimes. Can't get no job."

"You should have been nicer to those bums," I said. "I thought you got along with the homeless people."

"They're all a bunch of assholes," he said. "They don't like me because I've got a boat to sleep in."

"What about the law?" I asked. "You staying out of trouble?"

"I haven't been arrested, if that's what you mean," he answered. "But that water cop, Officer Kennedy, he's out here almost every day harassing me. He's over there in the mooring field too. Those people are just minding their own business."

"Did you happen to notice a new boat come into the mooring field yesterday?" I asked.

"Dude used to be in the marina," he said. "Cheap little sailboat."

"That's the one," I said. "I've got a bone to pick with that guy."

"You want me to go kick his ass?" said John. "I'd do it for a little cash."

"I think we decided that we didn't want to hurt him," I said. "But I've got no problem sinking his boat."

"I can do that too," he said. "I don't give a shit. I need to eat, man. Let me do it."

"Do you mind if I interject here?" asked Holly.

"Of course not," I answered. "Go right ahead."

"I know how you always just jump in with both feet," she said. "It's your style. I get it. But don't you think maybe this should involve a little planning? You've got a cop out here all the time watching things. You've got a desperate drunk getting involved, no offense John. Let's just take a breath and think things through."

"No offense taken," said John. "Everybody know I'm no good around here."

"Point taken, Holly," I said. "You're right. We need to get a look at his boat without him seeing us. Make sure he's not on board. Put together a strategy of some sort."

We all sat down and ate sandwiches and talked it over. John was a regular in the neighborhood. He didn't have any friends, but he could move about without raising any suspicions. He also had a bike on shore. I gave him my binoculars with instructions to scope out our target from the fishing pier and report back later. I promised him a decent dinner, along with a few beers. He was happy to do it.

"How can you trust that guy?" Holly asked.

"I do and I don't," I answered. "He wouldn't steal from me. He's likes me. I wouldn't want to rely on him in a pressure situation though."

"He's got crazy eyes," she said. "The dude's crazy, Breeze."

"You should see him when he's drunk," I said.

"We don't need his help," she said. "You need to get rid of him."

"I'll give him dinner and a couple of beers and send him on his way," I said. "Let's see what he finds out."

We cooked up cheeseburgers and opened a new bag of chips when John got back. Theren's boat was the last one in the row closest to the marina. He'd been aboard all afternoon. He didn't have a dinghy, but a blue kayak was strapped to the aft end of his boat. John guessed that he hadn't been to shore yet. If he had, the kayak would probably be in the water.

"Just let me go break his neck for you, Breeze," said John. "He don't look like much."

"No, no, no," I said. "I want to catch him off the boat and sink it. He'll be screwed proper and he'll know who did it."

"Suit yourself," he said. "If you change your mind, you know where to find me."

I cut John off after three beers. I gave him forty bucks and sent him home. I noticed he didn't go back to his boat. He went to shore instead. He was most likely headed for the liquor store. Holly and I tried to figure out the best way to proceed. We wanted Theren to be on shore while we took care of his boat, but we couldn't be seen. He couldn't know we were in town. We couldn't just walk over to the marina. He might be there on the docks. We also had the marine cop to worry about. Eventually, we decided we could sneak close at night. We'd look for the kayak. If it was gone, he was on shore. If it was with his boat, he was aboard. He wouldn't be able to see us in the dark. The water cop didn't patrol at night either.

I nursed a few beers while we waited for the sun to go down. I skipped the rum. I wanted to stay sharp. I couldn't see what might go wrong, but I had a nagging feeling about what was about to happen. Holly felt it too.

"Trust your gut," she said. "Something's not right about this."

"Let's make a dry run," I said. "We'll hide behind the bridge pilings, see what we can see. If it still doesn't feel right, we'll call it off."

"I don't want to go to jail over that little turd," she said.

"Me neither," I replied. "But I do want my revenge."

"What do you think is bothering us," she asked.

"Crazy John," I said. "Cross-eyed John, Drunk John, whatever his name is. He's a disturbance in the force. Messed up our mojo."

"He did kind of creep me out," she said.

"I'd like to tell you that he's harmless," I said. "But I know better."

We left at nine o'clock. If we waited too late he'd be sure to be on his boat. We passed John's boat and saw that he wasn't aboard. We went under the first bridge and moved towards the second. We weren't close enough to tell if the kayak was at Theren's boat or not. We idled about in the darkness, trying to get a feel for the night. My outboard noise was drowned out by the sound of cars on the bridge.

"What do you think?" I asked Holly.

"I can't see shit," she said. "I don't know."

"Let's get a little closer," I said. "I'll stay behind that big pole and those guide wires."

There's are huge poles that support power lines crossing the river where an old bridge used to be. The rubble from the demolition of the bridge makes a good fishing spot when the tide is right. That night, I used one of the poles to hide my approach. I couldn't get much further without being caught out in the open. I used very little throttle to move us through the water. It was slow, but it was relatively quiet. We were running without lights.

I grabbed a guide wire to stop our drift and shut down the outboard motor. Just as we got settled, the sky lit up with fire. In the new light we could see everything. Theren's boat was ablaze. It didn't explode, but it was burning brightly.

"Holly crap!" said Holly. "What just happened?"

"Let's go find out," I said.

I turned on our lights and fired up the motor. We went down the first row of mooring balls towards the flames. I saw someone go overboard from Theren's boat. I didn't see the kayak. I did see John's dinghy though. He stood on top of the cabin, pouring gasoline all over the deck. Flames surrounded him. He cackled like a madman as the fire spread. He was a madman, pure and simple. He was a drunken, stupid, mad, man. I yelled at him, but either he didn't hear or he didn't listen. Was he committing suicide? There seemed no way for him to escape. The boat was fully engulfed. I watched as he threw the gas can into the cockpit and dove through the flames to the water. I saw his hair briefly ignite before he splashed into the river.

He came up near the bow with a knife in his teeth. I watched again as he sawed through the boat's mooring line, setting it adrift. He swam to his dinghy next, cutting it free from the blazing wreckage. He climbed aboard and stood up in the small boat, surveying his handiwork.

Then we saw Theren in the water. His attempt at swimming wasn't going to keep him afloat for long. I motored over to him. He grabbed the side of the dinghy. Holly and I each grabbed an arm and lugged him over the side and out of the water. He fought to regain his breath, his eyes focused on the burning pile of fiberglass that used to be his boat.

We heard the sirens first, then saw the flashing lights of the fire and rescue boat. The marine patrol was right behind them. Cross-eyed John circled the burning heap in his dinghy. Fiberglass burns fast and hot. The vessel in question wasn't made of much. In minutes, the topsides were gone. It laid over on one side, dipping its mast in the river. What was left above the surface continued to burn until the whole mess sizzled and sank.

"I can't believe you sent that monster after me," said Theren.

"I didn't," I said.

"I don't think it's a coincidence that you show up just as my boat burns," he said. "I'm not that stupid."

"Long story," I said. "But I didn't send him after you."

The firemen and the cop pulled up to us and blinded us with light. Rapid-fire questions came from both. They made us all come aboard the fire boat, and took our dinghy in tow. The water cop rounded up John and brought him in as well. Back at the dock, chaos reigned. Theren started with accusations of kidnapping. John was so drunk he was incoherent. He tried to punch Theren but missed and fell. Theren changed his accusation mid-sentence. He combined the kidnapping with the arson of his boat. He sounded as crazy as John.

Holly and I kept our mouths mostly shut. We only spoke when spoken to. We addressed the questioners as sir. We were sober and calm. Finally, a deputy arrived from the sheriff's department. He knew John and his long criminal record. John went away in cuffs. Theren was put into a police car to settle down. That left me and Holly.

"You want to tell me what happened out there?" the officer asked.

"Crazy dude burned some other crazy dude's boat," I said. "Best I can figure."

"What were you two doing in the area at the time?" he asked.

"I have a friend that used to be on a mooring ball out there," I said. "We were looking for him, but I guess he's gone."

"I'd like to check that," he said. "You got a name and boat description."

"His name is Jeff Wilbanks," I said. "Older Chris Craft cabin cruiser. You can verify that with the marina, I'm sure."

"I'll do that," he said. "Now what's this about a kidnapping?"

"We had a run-in down in Fort Myers," I admitted. "His girlfriend decided she'd rather go live with her father than stay with him. I helped her get away."

"And it's just a crazy coincidence that you are here now?" he asked.

"Something like that," I shrugged. "I can give you the girl's father's number if you want."

"Great," he said. "I'll have to check that out too. Would you mind coming down to the station to fill out a statement?"

"I'd really rather not," I said. "I thought I was being a Good Samaritan pulling that guy out of the water. Now it's going to be a big hassle."

"Where's your boat?" he asked. "Are you in the marina?"

"We're anchored down by Fishermen's," I told him.

"If you don't want to make a statement," he said. "I'll have to ask that you don't leave town. I need to verify the information you've given me. Something just doesn't add up about all this."

"It's a crazy world we live in, officer," I said.

He took down Holly's phone number in case he had more questions. He did not ask for my boat name or description. It was late. He was frustrated. He should have taken us in and sorted out the whole thing, but he just wanted his shift to end. I imagined Cross-eyed John revealing my desire to sink Theren's boat. I figured Theren would pull himself together and better explain how I'd forcibly removed his girlfriend. Once again, a simple plan had evolved into a shit storm. Captain Fred would cover for me as best he could, maybe even make a few calls on my behalf. The marina would verify that a Jeff Willbanks had once been on the mooring field. John's testimony couldn't be relied upon. No matter how much sense Theren made, he'd have a hard time convincing the cops of his story.

"Screw them all," I told Holly. "Let's blow this place tonight."

"Where to?" she asked.

"Pelican Bay for starters," I said. "We'll get some rest and take off again tomorrow."

"By the time the cops figure that mess out," she said. "We'll be long gone."

"You learn fast, kiddo," I said.

We pulled up anchor and motored back down Charlotte Harbor in the dark. We tucked up deep in the mangroves on the south end of Punta Blanca Island, just in case anyone came looking for us. We went to sleep with no further discussion of the fiasco we'd left in our wake.

# Twelve

I woke to the chirping of ospreys. It was midmorning. The sun had risen well above the mangroves. Mosquitoes buzzed somewhere in my bunk. The events of the previous night weren't forgotten, but they were so bizarre as to seem unreal in the morning light. I'd unwittingly unleashed my crazy friend John on the hapless Theren. A very black comedy had ensued. Dealing with the cops was never my idea of a good time, even if I was innocent. This time, I wasn't entirely free from fault. There was enough truth mixed in with the ramblings to get me into hot water.

I'd come to Punta Gorda to sink a boat and get my revenge. I'd just have to call it mission accomplished and move one. The rest was collateral damage. No one had gotten hurt. The confusion of the deputy was almost amusing. I'd had worse outcomes. Holly didn't take matters so lightly.

"I know why you can't keep a women," she said. "Your life is nuts."

"Running coke never even got this messed up," I said. "It mostly went pretty smoothly."

"Mostly?" she asked.

"Sometimes things got hairy," I said. "But usually it was just running the boat, picking up packages, and bringing them back in."

"Did you ever have a run go bad?" she asked.

"It all started going bad at the end," I said. "Guys tried to steal our load. It involved bullets flying. Then rival dealers started moving in. I had to try to run them out of business while Bald Mark was in jail. I got out with my hide intact and a ton of money."

"That should have been enough," she said. "Now you're just pushing your luck with these dumb jobs."

"You're right, as usual," I said. "The voice of reason."

"Can't we just go back to beaches and blue water?" she asked.

"What about your boat?" I asked.

"We'll travel together," she said. "We'll explore the world, each in our own boat."

"We run about the same speed," I said. "Depending on the wind. It's doable."

"Let's go get my boat, then," she said. "Leave all this craziness behind."

We backtracked a little on our way out. We exited through the Boca Grande Pass and ran offshore. We went far enough out where we couldn't be seen from the beaches, or from small boats inshore. We were a tiny speck in a huge Gulf. If anyone was looking for us, we'd be hard to spot.

We turned south and rode the northerly breeze. The following sea was pleasant. It was the kind of passage that I loved. I wished Holly loved it as much as I did. Aboard my trawler, she never danced a jig, or removed her top. She didn't make passionate love to me like she'd done that day on her boat. I could sense her anticipation. She badly wanted to sail again. My consolation was that she hadn't decided to part ways. I'd been worried that once she got her boat in the water, she'd be gone forever. Instead, we'd worked out a compromise. I was happy for her.

We motored all day and all night. *Miss Leap's* engine purred me to sleep when it was Holly's turn to drive. I tinkered with wiring and connections along the way. By the time we got to Marathon, everything was back in working order. We passed under the Seven Mile Bridge and turned towards Boot Key Harbor. Holly was giddy with excitement. We passed the entrance to Marathon Boat Yard. Holly looked through binoculars, trying to spot *Another Adventure*. There was a sailboat under tarps in the sling. I was sure that was it. Howie would want to put on a show.

Holly had the dinghy in the water before I was finished securing the anchor.

"Hurry up, Breeze," she yelled.

"I'm coming," I said. "Keep your pants on."

It was the first, and last time I ever told a woman to keep her pants on. Howie was waiting for us. So were a dozen workers. He'd done the same thing with my boat. When you committed him and his staff to refurbishing your vessel, you got the full royal treatment.

"Are you ready to see your boat?" he asked Holly. "I'll see you about the bill afterwards, Breeze."

"Oh my God, I'm so ready," said Holly. "Pull those tarps off her."

The guys worked together to slide off the covers. The lift operator lowered her boat slightly. Someone brought a ladder. It was a work of art. The finished product was of showroom quality. It looked like a million bucks. I hoped it didn't cost that much.

Holly stood in wonderment. I thought back on our time together. She hadn't cried when her boat got ruined. She hadn't cried when I was near death. She'd always been a cool customer. Now, she cried. She bawled in front of all of us. She hugged me so hard I thought my ribs would crack. Howie cleared his throat behind us. She hugged him even harder.

"I can't believe it," she said. "It's so beautiful."

"Wait until you see the inside," said Howie. "Go ahead, climb on up."

He motioned me to follow him to his office. He picked up the work orders and final bill and handed them to me. It was just south of a hundred grand.

"Every penny well spent," he said. "Just like I did for you. Not another boat like it anywhere now."

"You did great," I said, shaking his hand. "You did a damn fine job. Holly's happy. That's all that matters."

"I hope she makes you happy later," he said. "That's a lot of dough for somebody else's boat."

"Only because you're such a crook," I said.

"Who you calling a crook?" he said. "You dope running jackal."

"It's fine," I told him. "Cash is on the boat. I'll run out and get it. Might take a while to count it all."

"I'll lower her down when she's ready," he said.

I went back out to the boat alone. I hadn't been alone on her for months. I opened a beer while counting out the bills. I was taking a serious hit to my piggy bank. I stuffed the money in a duffel and took my beer to the aft deck. I needed to sit and think for a minute. What had my life become? Where did I want it to go? Holly and I were partners, even lovers, but actually being in love hadn't happened for either of us. It had been the same with Joy. I'd probably still be with her if she hadn't been killed. Was it me, or was it the women? Maybe it was both. If you live long enough, you get burned. Your heart can only take so much pounding. We all find a way to protect ourselves. As a result, we never fully give of ourselves. I made that mistake with Andi. Back then I was still so full of grief. Sometimes, I kicked myself for letting her get away. Other times, I knew it wouldn't have worked at the time. I'd come through a lot since then. Now I had Holly to consider. If we were to part ways, now was the time. She had her boat. I had mine. This was our crossroads. We could say goodbye without it ever going bad for us. We'd have our memories, and they'd be good ones.

I didn't have the courage to broach the subject with her. Not now. She'd be one happy girl tonight. There was no sense in messing that up. I looked up and saw her coming out of the boatyard. *Another Adventure* sparkled in the sun. She motored right alongside me and shouted across.

"I'm going for a sail," she said. "I'll never forget this, Breeze."

She veered off and went through the bridge,

out towards the open ocean. I watched until I couldn't see her, then opened another beer. This is what it would be like. One day she'd sail away forever.

I went back to settle up with Howie. Some of the crew were still around. I thanked them all personally. They made a few jokes about me being a cradle robber. I heard how hot the rasta chick was. Howie was proud of himself, and his men.

"You taking good care of your boat, Breeze?" he asked. "I'd hate to see you tear her up like you done that one."

"She's fine as frog hair," I told him.

I didn't have the heart to tell him about her almost sinking, or the now-repaired bullet holes.

"Let's keep it that way," he said. "Even if you are sending my kids to college."

I went back to the boat and drank more beer, waiting for Holly. She sailed for hours. I pictured her out there naked, dancing a jig. She came back in at sunset, under full sail. She slalomed through the anchored boats like an America's Cup contestant. She fell into the wind, singlehandedly dropped the sails, and laid out her anchor. She had to start the motor to back down and set the hook. It was a fascinating display of true skill. I applauded on my bow, as loudly as I could.

She whistled and motioned for me to come over. I was happy to oblige. As soon as I got on board, she dragged me inside. She held me in a long, passionate embrace. She gave me a long, passionate kiss. We made long, passionate love. It was everything that lovers could be together. It was even better than when we done it under sail. Any thoughts of suggesting we go our separate ways were forgotten.

"She's perfect, Breeze," she said. "I'm blown away."

"That was the hot sex, my dear," I said.

"That blew me away too," she said. "How come you're so good to me?"

"I care about you deeply, Holly," I said. "You're the best friend I've ever had since my wife. Best lover too, when you want to be."

"I have a hard time letting myself go," she said. "You've manage to pry me loose twice now."

"I'd love to take all the credit," I said. "But it's this boat that gets you off."

"I didn't just have sex with myself," she said.

"Good point," I said. "It must be my awesome talents in the sack."

"I might need another test drive," she said. "Before I buy that."

I did my best to impress. The Breeze Model 53 Sex Machine had a few miles on it, but it still ran fine. I explained that this was an as-is deal. There was no warranty implied. If I broke down, I couldn't be returned to the factory.

I slept very well, with Holly snuggled up to me all night long.

*Take it as it comes, Breeze. Be happy in the present.*

# Thirteen

We awoke with morning breath and the urgent need to pee. The spell was broken. Over coffee we kicked around possible travel itineraries. We decided that since we'd left off in Georgetown, we could go back and continue south from there. We could check in on Fred and his daughter too. I liked that idea. I hoped they'd reached some sort of common ground. I wanted to think that something good had come out of our fiasco with Theren.

Holly's boat was capable of sailing straight to the Exumas. I couldn't do that in my boat. I'd need fuel along the way and places to anchor at night. We broke out the charts and started laying out a plan. I'd been across to Andros once. I could do that again. It was a long trip by yourself, but it was doable. Then we hop around to the Exumas and work our way down through the out islands. We'd figure the rest out when the time came. It felt good to be free. Holly was particularly cheerful.

We felt we made a unique couple. She was a true sailor. I was a sworn power boater. Somehow, we'd make it work. We'd see the islands together, but with two boats.

"I'm am so ready to take off and get out in the blue," said Holly.

"You'll need food and water," I said. "Fuel and supplies too."

"So mundane," she said. "I want to snap my fingers and have all that done."

"It's all in the preparation," I said. "You'll have a lot better time knowing you're ready for anything."

"I need to refill my Bahamas SIM card too," she said. "I guess I better make a list."

We spent a few days making ourselves and our boats ready for long passages. We walked to the grocery store and called Bob Narley's Taxi to take us back to the dinghy dock. We ferried water jugs to fill our tanks. We got our holding tanks pumped out. When you're getting ready to go for a long period of time, the list seems endless. Eventually, you just have to assume you're ready and go. If you forgot something you'll just have to deal with it.

We declared ourselves ready on a Friday afternoon, but we couldn't leave until Saturday. I had a long-standing superstition. You couldn't start a voyage on a Friday. You could travel on Friday's. You just couldn't begin your trip on Friday. Holly played along. She wasn't the superstitious type. She even violated the "No Bananas" rule. We waited until after midnight, until it was officially Saturday. We pulled up anchors and left Boot Key Harbor behind.

There was a breeze out of the east as we moved up Hawk Channel. We weren't crossing that day, only moving north to stage and wait for good weather if necessary. We hadn't decided exactly where we'd anchor for the night. Holly called me on the VHF so we could discuss it. I wanted to cut back inside at the Channel Five Bridge. We could go up the inside to Pumpkin Key and cross via Angelfish Creek. Holly doubted she could make it through with her six foot draft. It was unclear on both my chart and my GPS. I went below and dug out an old guide book by Claibourne Young. He had discussed Angelfish Creek in great detail. It didn't look like Holly could use it as an entrance to the ocean. Inside, the depths were plenty deep, but there were shallow spots at either end.

Holly wanted to wait at Rodriguez Key instead. We'd be exposed to the east wind all night. It wouldn't be comfortable. We argued for a few minutes. Eventually we decided to split up. I'd take the calm route on the inside and wait at Pumpkin Key. She'd stay outside and rock and roll all night. We'd each depart at six in the morning. Once we made our way through the reef, we'd get in touch. I would be able to see her sails from many miles away.

She wanted the wind in her sails no matter how rough the waves. I just wanted a smooth ride, the less wind the better. I sat alone that night and shook my head. We hadn't even left Florida yet. Already we'd encountered differences. Her deep draft was great in blue water, but it was a handicap inshore. The anchorage I'd chosen was the superior choice, but she simply couldn't use it. I thought she'd have some problems in the Bahamas as well, but we'd cross that bridge when we came to it.

I checked the weather and turned in early. We were good to go in the morning. We'd discussed our first few legs and gone over the charts. Once we got checked in to the Bahamas, we'd regroup and plan further.

I was up well before sunrise. I was rested and ready. It wasn't fully light yet when my anchor was raised and I slowly entered Angelfish Creek. The current in there was wicked. I barely made four knots on my way through. I managed six knots once I was clear of the eastern mouth of the creek. I weaved my way through the reef and headed due east. As the sun rose, I saw Holly's main go up to my south. Her jib soon followed. We had less than ten knots of wind out of the south. I'd be faster than her unless a breeze picked up. The crossing was a good one. Holly never caught up to me but I didn't lose sight of her. We entered the Banks at South Riding Rock and continued towards the Northwest Channel. It would have been nice to just shoot for the northern tip of Andros, but the charts showed that it was impossible. The water north of Andros was barely water at all. We had to make a big dogleg to avoid running aground.

The wind strengthened a bit before dark. Holly came up behind me and close the gap to less than a mile. We anchored for the night just a bit north and due east of the Northwest Shoal Light. I called Holly on the VHF.

"Are you up for a drink?" I asked.

"If you're buying," she answered.

She dumped a kayak overboard and paddled over for a visit.

"How was it?" I asked.

"My boat is so awesome," she said. "I can't believe how great she sails. All the new rigging, new sails, clean bottom. Man she'll fly if you give her enough wind."

"How fast were you going when you were gaining on me?" I asked.

"I topped out at nine knots," she said. "But I can do better."

The sun was long gone. We sat in the dark with our drinks. I brought out some cheese and crackers. It felt weird to be anchored out in the middle of nowhere. I decided to turn on every light I had. I didn't want to get run over during the night. We quickly went over the route for the next day, before Holly returned to her own boat. She was so full of joy. The happiness just bubbled out of her. Her boat, and the restoration that I had financed, was the best thing that had ever happened to her. She was excited for adventures to come.

We had an easy leg in to Morgans Bluff the next day. We cleared in with Customs and Immigration without incident. The procedure was done through a funky little bar. The sign said. Willy's Water Bar, but everyone was calling it Willy T's. The nice folks there directed us to a grocery store, offered to get us a cab, and tried to sell us a fishing trip.

We got some conch fritters and looked over our charts. Outside of Andros, there was a reef. Beyond the reef was a super deep piece of sea known as the Tongue of the Ocean. It's a shelf that drops off from about seventy feet to over six thousand feet. The color change is extraordinary. Holly wanted to troll a few fishing lines as we crossed it. I wished her luck, and put in my order for some fresh Mahi. We discussed what to do about Nassau. We'd skipped by it last time. Neither of us cared much for the cruise ship crowd. Holly said she didn't care to see it this time either. Once she got her sails up, she wanted to keep going.

The next day we left, crossed the Tongue of the Ocean, rounded New Providence Island, and anchored at Rose Island. We found a little beach bar called Sandytoes. We listened to music and watched the tourists. Whenever we were around other people, like back at Willy T's or there at Sandytoes, Holly's mind was off someplace else. She didn't say much. I assumed her thoughts were on open water sailing. She'd had a little taste of it, but we were just getting started. It was still a long way to Georgetown, and we'd seen it all before. She wanted to keep going south and explore new waters. I was with her, to a point. I'd already been as far as the British Virgin Islands. I knew what it took to get there. If she wanted to go south from there, it would all be new to me.

When we left the beach bar, she went back to her boat. I was beginning to not like this two boat situation. I laid in my bunk alone and tried to figure out where this new adventure would lead. I'd spent a lot of money to make her happy. Being with her made me happy. So far the weather had been excellent. The boats were performing wonderfully. Still, something bothered me. I puzzled over it for hours. Finally, I gave up and drifted off to sleep.

The run from Rose Island down to Allans or Highbourne Cay was a short one. We opted to skip them, as well as several other stops we'd already seen. We made our way to Hawksbill Cay instead. We were able to pick up mooring balls there. The place was surrounded by great beaches with soft white sand. We stayed an extra day to look around. We walked the beach together. It seemed like ages since we'd just strolled along at the water's edge. The voyage had taken precedent over shore-side activities. Traveling every day can get nerve wracking. I needed some time to relax and regroup. We'd been lucky with the weather too. It wouldn't hold out forever.

Holly was affectionate with me there on the beach. We held hands and she'd lean on me from time to time. The human touch was nice. I managed to coax her back to my boat that night. We shared a bed and broke our dry spell. The last time, the day she saw her boat, had been out of this world. This time it was gentle and sweet. She could be very loving at times.

"Are you happy, Holly?"

"I am happy," she said. "My mind is so full of things to come. The whole world is out there waiting."

It dawned on me then. The previous night I couldn't figure it out. I didn't want to sail around the world. I didn't want to see the seven seas. I wanted to settle down on some island with the perfect woman. I wanted peace and serenity. I'd had my share of adventures. In lieu of fulfilling that dream, I'd turned to taking on missions. It felt good to have a purpose. It gave me something else to focus on besides lying on a beach with a beautiful babe. Holly and I were so damn close to being what I wanted. We were kindred spirits in so many ways, but settling down in some quiet cove was not what she wanted. She was a lot younger than me. She'd just gotten started on her adventures.

This was not my mission or my dream. It was hers.

We left Hawksbill and jumped all the way down to Musha Cay. There we found a private island resort that we learned was owned by David Copperfield, the famous magician. We anchored on the western side in ten feet of water. We ate dinner together and poured over the charts again, trying to decide which cut to use to get to Elizabeth Harbor. Her boat's deep draft made these decisions very important ones. We settled on Adderley Cut. There were some rocks and coral heads, but they were charted and visible. There was plenty of depth to accommodate Holly's boat.

I didn't want to leave the next day. I saw wind and waves that I'd just as soon miss out on. Holly saw a chance for an extraordinary sail. We didn't argue. We calmly discussed.

"I'll get beat all to hell out there," I said. "It's nice here. What's another day?"

"*Another Adventure* is itching to spread her wings," she said. "It will be an epic sail."

"You'll have to go without me," I said.

"I can do it alone," she said. "I can read a chart. I don't want to miss this chance. Tomorrow it will be dead calm."

"Exactly," I said. "*Miss Leap* loves dead calm."

"I don't want to motor all the way to Georgetown," she came back. "I'm going today."

"I'll meet you there tomorrow afternoon," I said.

"Dinner on my boat," she said. "I'll fix something nice."

I watched her board *Another Adventure*. She

didn't start the engine. She took the sail covers off and raised the main. She pulled up anchor. As it came up off the bottom, her boat laid over in the wind and drifted to port. She ran back to the cockpit, yanked on some lines, and gained control. She sailed out of the harbor without ever using her motor. It was impressive. It really wasn't my thing, but I had to give her credit. She knew how to handle a sailboat.

There I was alone again, unless David Copperfield was home. I'd seen a small plane land on the island earlier in the day. Holly was out there having a sail-gasm without me. Good for her, I guess. Hopefully, I could nail her down for a few days in Georgetown.

# Fourteen

I had a nice smooth ride down to Georgetown, just the way I liked it. I dodged a delivery boat on my way in and passed just off the beaches of Stocking Island. At volleyball beach, I saw Holly standing at the water's edge. She was waving and smiling. After I passed, she went back to her volleyball game. She looked so youthful and energetic. I felt the need for a nap.

I anchored along Sand Dollar Beach and did just that. I shut my mind off and had a satisfying sleep. I was hoping the extra energy would be needed later on. By dinnertime, Holly hadn't shown up. I put my dinghy in and went off to see if she was on her boat. No one was home. I continued on to Volleyball Beach. I found her sitting at the Chat 'n Chill bar, drinking a beer with some folks near her age. She introduced me to the gang. Her face was red. I assumed it was from wind burn and not from embarrassment.

"The guys were just telling me there's a pig roast here on Sunday," she said. "We should come."

"Sure," I said. "It will be nice to sit still for a few days."

"Did you talk to Captain Fred?" she asked.

"I wanted you to go with me," I said. "Fred fell in love with you the last time."

"Sure," she said. "I liked him. Want to go visit tomorrow?"

"That's what we came her for," I said.

"Great," she said. "Pick me up around noon."

Then she finished her beer, got up, and returned to the volleyball court. Along with the younger people, there were a few guys older than me out there. I didn't want any part of it. I envisioned twisted ankles and sore muscles. I ordered a beer and watched the show. My bar mates were the wives of the old guys playing volleyball. Every time I looked their way, I caught them staring at me. I was the new kid in town to them.

Eventually, the game broke up and we ordered burgers.

"I thought you were going to fix me something nice," I teased.

"Shit, sorry about that," she said. "I got carried away over here. Forgot all about it."

"Fred will probably fix us a gourmet meal tomorrow," I told her. "Bring your appetite."

"You think his daughter will still be pissed at us?" she asked.

"Most likely," I answered. "But Fred will be happy to see us. Especially after what we did for him."

"Think of all the bullshit that followed," she said. "That was a nightmare."

"It's all behind us now," I said. "Shit worked out."

"You always say that," she laughed.

"It's true isn't it?" I said.

"Yea, I guess it is," she said. "Look where we are now."

"Okay if I stop by your place for a little quality time?" I asked.

"I don't know, Breeze," she said. "I'm pretty beat. Plus I'm all sweaty and dirty."

"Some other time," I said. "No problem."

I went back to my boat alone, again. First it was the sailing. Then it was younger people to play with. She was clearly having the time of her life, but I really wasn't. There I was in Georgetown for the umpteenth time, about to head off to who knew where. At least I should have been getting laid regularly. I skipped the beer and went straight for the rum. Rum never turned me down. I knew that once I opened the bottle, reasonable thinking and logic would soon become impossible. I wanted to sit and think, but I wanted the rum more.

My train of thought held for a good thirty minutes. That's when the edges started getting fuzzy. Before I quit, I came to some conclusions. At some point on that voyage, we'd come to a fork in the road. One of us would decide to go our separate way. I didn't know if it would be me, or if it would be her. I did know that I wasn't ready for that to happen yet. I gave in to the rum and started thinking about Holly's firm boobs and cute little butt. I wished she was there with me, but she wasn't. It was just me and my boat. That's how it always ended up. That's probably how it would end up this time too.

Holly was full of cheer when I picked her up the next day at noon. She'd cleaned up and put on nicer clothes. She had one small red ribbon tied into one of her dreads. She smelled nice. We chatted during the long dinghy ride to Red Shanks. She wanted to go into town after we left Fred's boat.

Fred was beside himself when we arrived. He treated us like royalty. I didn't see his daughter anywhere.

"How are things with her?" I asked, meaning his daughter.

"It's going to be okay, Breeze," he said. "She was a pissy thing when she first got here, but I've made a few small steps to make amends."

"Where is she?" I asked.

"She doesn't want to see the two of you," he said. "She's in her cabin, moping."

"She knows that we were acting on your orders," I said. "And in her best interest."

"That's not the issue anymore," he said. "It's what happened with her boyfriend afterwards that's stuck in her crawl. She made it sound like it was World War Three down there."

"It practically was," said Holly. "Crazy people, burning boats. It was insane."

"You mean she's been in touch with him?" I asked.

"Talks to him all the time," said Fred. "Little fucker was sleeping under a bridge. She was out of her mind about it. I sent him some money to get an apartment. Made things better between her and me."

"Sorry things got a little out of hand," I said. "But he deserved it."

"I've got no qualms about it," he said. "You did what I asked you to do. Given the nature of the request, things were bound to get sticky. That's why I came to you. You've got a knack for sticky, although I did have to make some phone calls to the local sheriff's office."

"Thanks again, Fred," I said. "Bailing me out again."

"All part of the same job," he said. "No additional debts have been incurred. I'm grateful to you, Breeze. She and I are working things out."

"That's fantastic," I said.

"Hard to believe there could be a happy ending," said Holly. "I'm glad for you captain."

"And I'm glad that you are here to brighten my day, Holly," he said. "You're such a vibrant young lady. Too much for that old sea dog."

"On the whole you're right," I said. "But I have my days."

"I bet you do," he said. "String of beautiful women he's brought through this harbor. You know that don't you Holly."

"I've heard," she said. "I've even met one of them. Taylor was one of the hottest chicks I've ever seen."

"They were all beautiful in their own way," he said. "Just as you are young lady."

"I appreciate you pumping up my ego, Fred," I said. "But can we change the subject here?"

"Certainly," he said. "Let's discuss the meaning of life over fine wine and finer cigars."

The meaning of life for Fred was fine dining, good company, and his yacht. He'd lived a high-powered, stressful life until now. Everything he'd worked for had now come to fruition. He'd bitten and clawed his way to the top. Now he could enjoy the fruits of his labors.

"The two of you being here is a great pleasure to me," he said. "This is what I live for."

He motioned to Holly, signaling that it was her turn.

"I've just recently figured out my calling," she said. "The meaning of life is the wind in my sails. When the sails first go up, I'm an eagle. I'm crouching for takeoff. When they fill, I'm soaring through the sky. On my boat, out there on that awesome blue ocean, I'm totally free. That's what I live for."

"What about you, Breeze?" asked Fred. "Nomadic adventures on the high seas like young Holly here? A different woman in every port? You've lived a lot of life my friend. Certainly you've found some meaning in it."

I didn't want to tell them the truth. I would have told Fred if Holly wasn't in the room. I couldn't tell them that the meaning of life was completely and fully sharing your soul with another person. I couldn't say that finding true intimacy was the pathway to fulfillment. I was no philosopher. I'd screwed up my life ten ways to Sunday. I tried to be honest without going full-blown self-help guru.

"I've been through a lot and I've come a long way," I began. "Not that long ago I was eating out of cans, when I could afford to eat at all. I could barely grow enough weed to pay for the fuel it took to get me to town in order to sell it. Tonight, I'm sitting on a fancy yacht with two of the finest people I've ever met. What is the meaning of life? Hell if I know, but sharing it with the people you love is a good start."

"That's touching," said Fred. "But what's the end-game for Breeze?"

"He wants to waste his days with a beautiful woman on a Caribbean beach," said Holly. "Something like that."

"There's been plenty of beaches and plenty of pretty women," I said. "Holly, you're the best of them all, but it's something else."

"Does it have to do with what you had with your wife?" she asked. "You don't have to answer if you don't want to."

"I never met your wife, Breeze," said Fred. "Hard to picture you married. She must have really been something."

"It wasn't just her," I said. "It was us. Together we became whole. I can't explain it, but I guess that is the meaning of life for me."

"I've had two wives and a hundred girlfriends," he said. "But I never experienced that. You're a lucky man to have found it."

"Me neither," said Holly. "I thought I did, but it was all a lie."

Both of them sat there looking at me, like I was the keeper of life's great secret. I didn't know what else to say.

"I guess I'll settle for that beautiful woman on a Caribbean beach," I said. "Sounds like a pretty good life to me."

"To beautiful women," said Fred, raising his glass.

"And beautiful boats," said Holly.

"And wonderful friends," I said.

We clinked our glasses together and drank to the meaning of life.

# Fifteen

We stayed with Captain Fred all day. It was too late to go to town after we left. Holly asked if she could come aboard my boat. We watched the sunset together in silence. She led me to my bunk in silence. The silence was broken when we made love. We gave ourselves to each other as best we could. We sought something beyond what we already had. It was true and it was honest. We almost made it.

I took her to town in the morning to show her the lay of the land. We took the dinghy under a low bridge into Lake Victoria. We both would need provisions before continuing on our journey. We had coffee and pastries at the

Driftwood Café. We checked out the Exuma Markets where we had tied the dinghy. We noticed they had free water there for boaters. Continuing south on the main road, we located the laundromat, trash dumpsters, and another grocery store. We walked back the other way and over the bridge. We found the liquor store, a produce market, and the library.

The shopkeepers and other boaters that we encountered were all friendly. The town itself seemed to exist to cater to the boats in the harbor. It was much more American than the dusty little town in Luperon. Everyone spoke English. There were familiar brand names on the store shelves. You could get just about anything you wanted there, but the selection was limited. If you wanted soap, they didn't have fourteen different varieties. They had one. Same for shampoo, toilet paper, etc. No one stood in front of twenty different brand names of peanut butter, trying to decide. There was one brand only.

I wanted to stay for lunch. All the walking made me hungry. Holly had other plans. She'd made a sailing date with Captain Fred. This was another big difference between sailors and power boaters. I never, ever, just took my boat out for a joyride. Once I had a good anchor set, I was staying put until it was time to move on. Holly would pull up anchor at a moment's notice just to go out and ride the wind. I dropped her off and returned to my vessel. I made a sandwich and watched her sail off the anchor again. She was showing off for Fred. I used my free time to fill my water tanks. I ferried jugs back and forth from the Exumas Markets dinghy dock until my big tanks were full.

I used the rest of the afternoon to run through all of my systems checks. After declaring everything shipshape, I cracked a cold one. I thought about the journey ahead. Other than a few small settlements, there was little civilization between Georgetown and the Turks and Caicos. If Holly and I were to cement our relationship and really come together, it would be on those empty and pristine beaches. Then we'd have long passages to busy places in front of us. The Dominican, Puerto Rico, and the Virgin Islands were down there waiting for us. How far would we go? How long until we parted, or would we stay together forever?

I considered all the things that could go wrong. One of us could have a major mechanical failure in some remote area. One of us could hit a reef and bust up our boat. One of us could decide that we've had enough. I didn't see Holly giving up. It was more likely that she'd tire of me and my slow boat holding her back. The trade winds down there are strong and steady. She'd be a rocket ship on the way south. I'd be willing to hole up in a protected anchorage to wait for a better day. She'd want to get out there and run with it.

The course ahead was fraught with peril, but that had never stopped me before. I'd invested myself in Holly. We were tied to this trip together. I'd ride it out as long as I could. We'd grow together or we'd grow apart. Shit would work out, for better or for worse.

*Another Adventure* sailed back into the harbor late in the afternoon. Fred had parked his dinghy on the beach, where Holly had taxied him out to her boat earlier. She took him back and he roared off through the anchorage towards Red Shanks. Holly came to me.

"We're having dinner at Fred's," she said. "He said to take separate dinghies. He wants to talk with you in private later."

She puttered off after him. I didn't know what to make of Fred's intentions. I shrugged and followed after the two of them.

We had another fine meal and more good conversation. Fred and Holly were best buddies now. Whenever she'd been around her elders before, she was always quiet and respectful. She didn't talk much. With Fred, she was completely comfortable. He'd made her feel at ease. It was well after dark when he motioned for her to run along. He turned to me after she left.

"She says that she wants to sail the world over," he said. "What are you going to do?"

"Try to keep up with her," I said. "Wouldn't you?"

"If I was younger," he said. "Of course I would."

"What is it that you wanted to talk to me about?" I asked.

"Holly was very open with me today, Breeze," he said. "She thinks the world of you, but she admits that something is not quite clicking all the way."

"She told you that?" I asked.

"In so many words," he said. "She doesn't know if you're both trying too hard or not trying hard enough."

"I wish I could figure it out myself," I said. "I think about it a lot. I don't think we're going to make it. I want us to, but it doesn't seem like it's going to happen."

"I've got no wisdom in these affairs," he said. "But I'm going to offer my help in a manner that I'm more accustomed to."

"What's that?" I asked.

"Money," he said. "There is a chance that Holly feels indebted to you for paying to fix her boat."

"She didn't ask me for a loan," I said. "I volunteered. She doesn't owe me anything."

"She's a free spirit," he said. "She may or may not have a nagging feeling that you've purchased her affections."

"That's ridiculous," I said.

"Maybe you feel that since you've spent so much money on her, that you'll stick it out even when it becomes unwise," he said. "Neither of you will ever be free of the financial contract you share."

"This isn't something that I've even considered," I admitted.

"That had to be a large blow to your cash reserves," he said. "Am I right?"

"It was a pretty good chunk," I said.

"How long before you run out of money?" he asked.

"I never think like that," I said.

"Maybe you should start," he replied.

"What is it that I'm getting here?" I asked. "Relationship advice or financial advice."

"You're getting money, son," he said. "I'm paying you for Holly's debt."

"Then won't she feel like she'll owe it to you?" I asked.

"I'm not sleeping with her, Breeze," he said. "Once she leaves this harbor, I'll probably never see her again."

"Then why are you doing this?" I asked.

"You two will both be free of that one nagging question," he said. "You might make it work. You might not, but it won't be the money that comes between you."

"Maybe you have more wisdom in these affairs than you think," I said. "Either that or you've got more money than sense."

"I've let money, or the pursuit of it, ruin every chance I ever had at a real relationship," he said. "You two are honestly seeking something that I'll never have. I want to give you every chance to find it."

"I don't know what to say," I said.

"Say thanks and take the damn money," he said. "Chase that girl like it means something to catch her."

"I will, Fred," I said. "Thank you doesn't seem like enough, but thanks."

He presented me with a huge stack of crisp one hundred dollar bills. I knew it wasn't that much money to him, but it was a king's ransom to me. My cash reserves were as full as they'd ever been. I'd have to find new ways to hide money on my boat. Oddly, I did feel a burden removed. I hadn't blinked when I'd paid all that money, but I fretted about it later. It was one less worry now. Hopefully, it would be one less worry for Holly as well.

I didn't go to her that night. I went home to *Miss Leap* and devised new nooks and crannies to hide cash. I knew every inch of her, but not every spot was dry. The best hiding places were down in the bilge gunk in some waterproof container. A coffee can wouldn't do. I finished stashing the cash and went out on deck. Holly was standing on hers. She waved. I waved back.

She stopped by the next day on her way to get water.

"How'd your talk go?" she asked.

"It's all good," I said. "All good."

"Cool," she said. "I'll catch up with you later."

She drove off towards town. We never mentioned the money again.

We met up at the Chat 'n Chill later in the day. Some college kids were playing volleyball, showing off their tattoos and strutting their stuff. After we ate, Holly joined in the game. One particular guy paid her a lot of attention, too much attention. I watched him find ways to touch her. At first, she seemed oblivious. I'd seen this in her before. She simply didn't realize how attractive she was. She was just playing volleyball, but this dude was looking for much more. He finally went too far and she tried to put a stop to it.

"Keep your hands to yourself, asshole," she said.

"Whoa," he said. "You calling me an asshole? You know you want some of this."

That's when I stepped in. I took her by the hand and led her off the court. He followed. I'd been watching him. He was muscular but not awkwardly so. His movements were fluid, like a cat ready to pounce. He was obviously athletic. He was also an arrogant jerk, so he'd probably been in his share of fights. I didn't want to mess with him. I just wanted to diffuse the situation. He had other ideas.

He shoved me hard from behind. If I wasn't holding Holly's hand, I might have fallen. It was going to go down whether I wanted it to or not. I looked around for something to use as a weapon. Beer bottles were strung about on the picnic tables. I grabbed one and swung it at him in one smooth motion. He blocked me with a forearm and gave me a quick jab in the gut. I bent down instinctively and saw his foot coming for my face. I was just able to move my head in time. His foot glanced off my ear. I still had the beer bottle in my hand. He was a little off-balance after the kick. I caught him just above the eye. He went down in the sand and I was on top of him. I put a thumb on his windpipe and pushed hard. I had the bottle over my head, ready to strike if necessary.

That's all I remember. Everything went black for me then. One of his pals clobbered me and the rest of them took turns using my head for a soccer ball. It took a dozen patrons of the bar to break up the melee. The frat boys laughed at the old man down in the sand as they were escorted away. No charges were filed. No police were called.

My feelings weren't hurt, but my head certainly did. I'd taken out the asshole fair and square. I should have known what would happen next. I should have tried harder to avoid the fight. Everything creaked and popped as Holly helped me to my feet. The bartender put some ice in a towel for my head. He put a beer in front of me. A couple of my saviors patted me on the back.

"Jesus, Breeze," said Holly. "I thought they were going to take your head off."

"Good thing they weren't wearing shoes," I said.

"Who gets in a fight sitting on a beach in the Bahamas?" she asked. "Christ."

"You made me people," I said. "I don't people very well."

"People suck," she said. "I get it, Breeze, but damn."

"Let's just leave here," I said. "Go where there ain't people."

"I'm ready after that," she said. "I've got to go shopping first, but I'm ready."

We each took on groceries the next day and met back at my boat to go over charts. I wanted to visit a little slice of paradise called Hog Key Cut. Only vessels with a draft of less than five feet can enter. That ruled out Holly. Instead, we could use the Comer Channel to access the Jumentos and the Ragged Islands. We decided to jump over to Long Island after that. We said our goodbyes to Captain Fred that night. He served us Duck a l'Orange over wild rice. He asked about our travel plans and we told him about our next few intended stops.

"Safety first," he said. "Keep an eye on the weather and don't take any foolish chances. Not much water around the Jumentos. Salt Pond is a good stop though. Anything goes wrong, you can call me from there. Further south, there's nothing."

To my surprise, Fred's daughter made an appearance just as we were about to leave.

"I want to apologize for being difficult," she said. "Dad was right to get me out of there. I'm going to be fine here. I even like it some. Theren is better off not living on that silly little boat."

Holly and I spoke simultaneously.

"Shit works out," we said.

# Sixteen

We explored the islands south of the Exumas. We found a deserted beach, and got back to the job of erasing our tan lines. Holly started diving again. Lobster were plentiful in the surrounding waters. Those waters were as clear and pretty as we'd ever seen. I fished assorted rock piles for snapper. We ate well and made love often. It was a glorious time for us. We were at our best away from the rest of the world. When it was just the two of us alone, everything was right. I didn't want it to end.

Eventually, we started running out of things. Neither of us had any bread or fresh fruits or vegetables. We dealt with it for a while, but when my beer supply got low, it was time to move on. We raised anchors, bound for Long Island. Salt Pond, is the best known anchorage on the island. Just north of the Salt Pond Bight, Indian Hole Point runs east to west out into the bank forming Thompson Bay. The first anchorage we tried was too shallow for *Another Adventure*. We backed off and regrouped. We moved into the lee of Evas Cay and gently picked our way to a spot with seven foot of water. The place was beautiful, but a good low tide would leave Holly's boat sitting on the bottom. We also shared the anchorage with several other boats.

We were able to get mangos, pineapples and bread on the first day. Hillside Grocery Store was well-stocked with bread and necessities. On the second day I discovered the liquor store just to the north of the grocery. I paid sixty dollars a case to refill my beer supply. I had no choice. I wasn't going to go without beer for the rest of the trip.

Over dinner we discussed our next move. Things were about to change. Most cruisers will tell you that it's different south of Georgetown, and it's true. We were about to cross the Tropic of Cancer. Below that line, you're in the

Tropics, not the sub-tropics. Below that line the water is a whole different story. You are exposed to the Atlantic Ocean. There are epic passages to make. There aren't many all-weather anchorages. There's hardly any settlements and no place to get fuel.

Holly's boat would really come into its own there. Mine, not so much. Her deep draft had been a hindrance to us so far. Now, it would be a great asset as we took on heavier seas. My slow and stable trawler really wasn't built for these types of passages. I had confidence in my vessel and in my abilities, but I wasn't looking forward to the coming days.

The next destination was the Crooked Islands. We had a decision to make. The shortest route forward to the Turks and Caicos called for us to navigate around the eastern side of the island. Generally, the weather is incoming from the Atlantic Ocean, from east to west. We'd be exposed to that for a long time. Shelter looked hard to come by if things got hairy. It made a lot more sense to me, to use the longer, western route. The land mass would provide shelter from the easterlies, and there were more anchorages in which to seek refuge. On the other hand, it would create a really long passage to Mayaguana, or even the Dominican. I really didn't like either option. If the weather was calm, neither would be a problem, but any foul conditions at all would make the trip unbearable.

"Think ahead," said Holly. "If you want a decent run to the Turks, we need to go east. We have a risky leg sooner or later. Let's choose the shortest risk."

"We could go from the south end of the Acklins over to Mayaguana," I suggested.

"'We' be slogging due east," she said. "Into the trades. That would suck."

"You're right," I said. "If we jump off from North East Point, we'll have a southeast heading."

"I'll have a good point of sail," she said.

"And I'll be taking a beam sea," I said.

There was really no compromise. In the end, I let Holly have her way. We'd go over the top of the Crooked Islands and round them to the east. We'd head south inside the Plana Cays, then veer off to Mayaguana. *Miss Leap* and I were in for a rough couple a days.

The trip to Bird Rock, at the northern tip of the

Crooked Islands, was only thirty-five miles. The weather was good. We made Portland Harbour in the early afternoon. It wasn't really a harbor at all. It was just a ring of circling reef. The ocean swells rolled over the reef and rocked the anchorage. We moved in as close to shore as our drafts would allow in an attempt to gain settled water. Unless the winds decreased, we'd have an uncomfortable stay. If they got worse, we'd be sorry to be stuck there.

While we were looking over the charts that afternoon, it did indeed, get worse. Our boats were rolling and jerking on their anchor chains. My beer slid off the chart table and spilled on the salon floor. That was enough. Holly went back to her boat. We immediately pulled up our anchors and continued down the coast. It was even worse out on the open Atlantic, but we needed better shelter for the night. Just a few miles south, we found a better spot to anchor. We chose a place off a white sand beach halfway between Landrail Point and Pittstown Point. We anchored in deep water, well-protected from the east winds. I don't know how we missed this anchorage during our earlier study. I was frazzled from the trip. I was hungry. We needed good weather information. This wasn't fun.

We found Mrs. Gibson's Lunch Room on shore. We got some fresh bread and internet access. Holly looked over the forecast. The easterlies would continue. They were not forecast to be too strong for Holly, but I didn't like them. She wanted to jump down to Atwood Harbor in the Acklins. I preferred to make a shorter hop to French Wells. This time, I won the argument. I'd given in to her on the last decision. She had to go along with my choice.

We tried to make it into French Wells the next day. I didn't have a problem. The channel was bordered by shoals on either side. I slowed down and felt my way in. Once inside, the depth increased. It was an excellent anchorage with protection from any wind direction. I watch Holly slow down at the entrance. She was glad to be moving slowly when she ran aground. She hailed me on the radio as she attempted to back off. She managed to free herself. She swung around for another pass at it. She bumped the bottom again.

"Shit, Breeze," she said. "I don't think I can get in."

"The tide is half out," I said. "It's only going to get tougher. You could have made it at high tide."

"Well, why didn't we time it for the high then?" she asked.

"The chart shows ten feet," I answered. "It must have shoaled in."

"Where's the next anchorage?" she asked.

"Atwood," I said.

"We should have gone there in the first place," she said. "I'm going to have to keep going. I can make it before dark. You coming with?"

"I'm tired, Holly," I said. "I'd like to rest."

"It's not that far," she said.

"It wasn't that long ago I got my head kicked in," I said. "It wasn't long before that I had some Bahamian witch doctor putting shit on my back to save my ass. I'm beat. I'll meet you there tomorrow."

"Sorry, Breeze," she said. "I'll wait for you at Atwood. Take whatever time you need."

She reversed course and went back out into the Atlantic. I felt old. I didn't want us to be apart, but I didn't have it in me to follow her that day. I let her go on without me. It was a foreboding feeling. Someday she might go on without me, and never come back. I laid on the settee and licked my wounds. I needed to learn to avoid flying rigging, and college boys with attitudes.

When I woke up, the winds were still blowing. I was safe and sound in a snug harbor, but Holly was many miles to my south. I pulled my sorry ass out of bed and made some coffee. If I wanted to catch up with her, I'd have to slog out into the Atlantic and beat my way to her. I wasn't looking forward to it, but I resigned myself to another long day at sea.

*Come on, Miss Leap. Time to chase the girl.*

It was every bit as bad as I'd feared it would be. The seas were running eight to ten feet offshore. The waves were widely spaced, but I couldn't get into a rhythm with them. Every third one would catch us funny and send shudders through the hull. Salt spray covered the enclosure, making it hard to see. We pounded and plunged for what seemed like eternity. Eventually, I picked up a waypoint on my GPS marked ATWOD. I ran to it and saw a crescent-shaped bay with no markers. I had to pay close attention getting in. There was coral strewn about in no particular order. I saw Holly's boat, and drew close to it. I pulled up short, dropped the anchor, and made sure it was set firmly.

I was even more worn out than the day before. The constant voyaging was taking its toll. I'd been this way before, but the weather had been favorable then. We still had several tough legs in front of us. I didn't even know where we were going after the Virgin Islands. I'd taken a terrible beating on the south coast of Puerto Rico the last time I went that far. Andi was with me on that trip. I'd taken my wife's ashes to Norman Island. Andi helped me get through it. I hadn't thought of her in a long time. The last I knew, she was living in Luperon. She'd opened a small clinic to help the local children. Holly and I would be visiting Luperon in the near future. I wondered if Andi was still there. Seeing her again would complicates things for me and Holly. I didn't need any more complications.

Holly pulled alongside in her dinghy. She looked clean and well rested. She gave me a big smile.

"Glad to see you made it," she said. "Everything okay?"

"It was a rough ride for us," I said. "*Miss Leap* and I didn't enjoy it."

"What do you think about the next leg?" she asked.

"You got any weather information?" I asked.

"Still east, but dropping to ten to fifteen," she said.

"The trip to Mayaguana is only about forty miles," I said. "We can tuck in at Abraham Bay and be out of the wind."

"So you'll be ready to roll in the morning?" she asked.

"No rest for the weary," I responded.

"Get some sleep," she said. "I'll whip up some breakfast in the morning. You'll be good as new."

She left me there alone. I watched her go and thought about our endgame. We'd break no intimacy barriers living like this. We'd have to get some place safe and stop for a while. We needed to really sit down and talk about it, find out what we wanted out of this deal. I almost wished for some bad weather to come along and keep us stuck in port. Then maybe we could sort things out.

I was too tired to cook for myself. I made a sandwich and drank one beer before dozing off. I saw *Another Adventure* in a dream. It was in front of me as I stood on the bridge of *Leap of*

*Faith*. We were underway and I was losing ground. I pushed my old boat to it limits, but still fell further behind. Eventually, Holly's boat disappeared over the far horizon. I gave up. I slowed down gradually until I was stopped. I drifted for a bit, before turning back. Where was I going back to? It wasn't clear. The dream ended. There was just the soft rolling waves of the ocean left. There was nothing out there but endless blue.

Sometimes, dreams are just dreams. Other times, they might be your subconscious trying to speak to you in your sleep. They are manifestations of what's been on your mind. Outwardly, I hadn't given up yet. I think Holly believed that I'd follow her to Tierra del Fuego if she asked. She'd drag me and my old boat around Cape Horn, fighting off pirates along the way. Inside, I knew I couldn't do it. I didn't want to do it. I'd given up control of my own destiny. That could not continue. I couldn't continue.

I'd have to come up with the courage to tell her. I'd have to find the right time.

In the morning, the winds have subsided to a reasonable level. It looked to be an easy crossing. Holly whipped up lobster omelets. She had some fresh pineapple to go with it. The day was sunny and bright, as was Holly's disposition. This life was agreeing with her. She was in her zone and happy about it. Her lightness of spirit rubbed off on me and improved my mood. Seeing her happy made me happy.

We set out together at ten. The seas were slowly rising at three to four feet. There were no breakers or whitecaps. We traveled southeast for six hours until we approached Mayaguana. We stayed clear of Devil's Point. It sounded like a bad place to be. We swung well wide of it to the south. Then we turned back north and made our way into Abraham Bay. I'd been in there before. There are some tricky reefs that you can see if you're paying close attention.

I tried to remember the lay of the land from my prior visit. There was a fairly wide opening in the first reef we encountered, but then there was a secondary reef, lying right in our path. I almost got trapped the last time by trying to cut between the second reef and Guano Point. That was a mistake. Instead, we ran northwest, leaving the reef to starboard. The depths got as shallow as eight feet. I went slowly, and Holly followed. By the time we got our anchors down, we had just under seven feet of water. It was a pretty skinny place for Holly to be. On the plus side, it was protected from the prevailing wind. The bay was calm. It was a good spot to spend the night.

We had fresh fish for dinner, with some sort of mango salsa. Holly wanted to know all about the Turks and Caicos, The Caicos Banks, the DR and the Mona Passage. She was way ahead of me. I was just happy to be tucked into a calm bay. After dinner, we sat on deck and watched the sun go down. Holly leaned on me as the last of its light blinked out. We made love right there under the evening sky. It was not a good time to discuss parting ways.

Instead we figured out the next leg of our journey. It would be a fifty mile run down to the Sandbore Channel. This would get us into Sapadillo Bay, just off Provo. We'd have to clear Customs before moving any further. We could get a feel for the weather there, but it would be the last place to get an internet connection. The Caicos Banks would have to be run in the daylight hours, with good weather conditions. It had coral heads and shifting sand bars that would present frequent obstacles. It was nothing to mess around with. I explained all this to Holly, using my finger to point out waypoints on the chart. She understood everything I said. She'd come a long way as a navigator on this trip. She watched me constantly, studying my decision making process. She often perused charts in our downtime.

"Weather is the key from here on out," I told her. "Keep your eyes on the sky, and your barometer. Feel for the smallest change in the air."

"The farther we go, the more cautious you get," she said. "What happened to Wing It Breeze?"

"You can't half-ass anything in the Tropics," I said. "Those trade winds, the current, coral heads and squalls, you need to respect them all."

"Aye-aye, captain," she said.

The weather was turning in our favor, at least for a few days. We had an easy ride down to Provo. First we anchored, but found that no Customs agent was available to check us in. Holly made a few calls. The Blue Haven Resort and Marina could accommodate us, and it was a recognized entry point. There was a fifty dollar fee to check in, and a fifty dollar fee to leave.

We paid them both at the same time. This only gave us permission to remain in the country for one week. If we planned to stay longer, the fee went up to three hundred dollars. We only needed a few days.

We took advantage of what the marina had to offer. We got our holding tanks pumped out and washed the salt off our boats. There was a bar on site. After our chores we went up to have a few drinks. We encountered people. They were mostly boaters, with a few tourists mixed in. We didn't stay long.

We left the next morning, bright and early. The Caicos Banks were almost seventy miles wide. We wanted to whole run to be done in the daylight. I instructed Holly not to follow me too closely. If I ran up on some coral she needed to be able to react in time to avoid collision. We bobbed and weaved our way all day long. We reached Big Sand Cay, at the southernmost tip of the Turks and Caicos, well before dark.

Big Sand Cay is an uninhabited island and a protected bird sanctuary. I'd never gone ashore there. I thought you might need special permission. Besides, I'd been on the run from the law my last time here. I didn't want to encounter any park rangers or other law enforcement. We anchored in twelve feet of water over a white sand bottom. The weather was settled. It had been a ten hour day. A more ambitious sailor might have decided to continue on towards the Dominican. Good weather should be taken advantage of. I didn't have that kind of ambition. I didn't bring it up. Neither did Holly.

Then we sat down for our nightly planning session and she figured it out for herself. We wanted to arrive in Luperon early in the morning. The winds kick up by mid-morning. You can't enter the harbor in the dark for two reasons. Local fishermen string nets across the harbor entrance at night. It's also a tricky navigational problem. You need light to pick your way in. Five o'clock in the evening would be the time to go. Right then would have been smart actually. I just didn't want to. I'd already had a long day underway. We'd have to stay over almost the entire next day before we departed.

Holly understood, but I could tell she was itching to get moving. I explained to her that we were about to cross eighty or ninety miles of the Atlantic at its worst. The trades kept it churned up. It was big water, deep and sometimes dangerous. It wouldn't be a joyride. I taught her a trick I'd learned the hard way. We'd be traveling south, but if the east winds pushed too hard, you could roll with them and make landfall to the west of Luperon. I showed her La Isabela, just to the west, and Punta Rucia, further down the coast. If necessary, run to safe harbor at either of those bays, I told her. Leave before sunrise and get to Luperon before the winds come up. It would be calm along the north coast for a few hours in the early morning.

We finished our studies and retired for evening drinks.

"I've been wondering something," she said.

"What's on your mind?" I asked.

"If and when you're going to bail on me," she said.

She had more courage than I did. She went there. It caught me off guard.

"It's been on my mind, to be honest," I said. "I haven't reached any conclusions."

"Same here," she said. "Don't you think we ought to talk about it?"

"I've been putting it off," I said. "I don't want to think about not being with you."

"I can't bear the thought of it either," she said. "But we both know it's coming."

"There doesn't seem to be any compromise," I said.

"Are you willing to leave your boat and come sail with me?" she asked.

"You know the answer to that," I said.

"You'll never leave that boat," she said. "And you're not that keen on sailing, except for the sex part."

"And you won't part with your boat either," I said. "Not that you should. We just have different dreams. The meaning of life is different for each of us. We discussed this."

"Then why did you come along?" she said. "Why did you come this far?"

"Just to be with you," I said. "I don't want to let go."

"Me neither," she said.

She started to cry. She came to me and hugged me. She didn't stop crying as she undressed.

She put her head on my chest and cried while I undressed. For the first time, we gave ourselves completely. We let go of whatever had been holding us back. It was love and it was passion. It was tenderness and caring. It was intimate, the real deal. Only in knowing that we wouldn't stay together, were either of us able to fully let go. It was a damn shame, and it made Holly start to cry again.

"We could have been so wonderful together," she sobbed.

I was afraid that if I spoke, I'd cry too. I held her close, gently rocking. I was letting another good one get away. I was a thousand miles from nowhere, with no place to go. Soon, I'd be alone. I couldn't imagine being any sadder.

Holly pulled herself away, wiping her eyes. She pulled herself together as we dressed.

"I've interrupted your dreams long enough," she said. "You'll make someone very happy on that island of yours. Take her to the Berry's."

# Seventeen

We had a day to kill. We walked the beach, hand in hand. There was no one else on earth.

"What are you going to do now?" she asked. "Where will you go?"

"Short term, I'll stay with you to Luperon," I said. "After that, I have no clue."

"Why?" she asked. "Why not turn back instead of beating all the way to the DR?"

"I like Luperon," I said. "I've got some memories there. An old friend who might still be around."

"A lover?" she asked.

"We tried twice," I said. "Didn't work out either time. I haven't thought about her in a long time. Seems silly to come this close and not look her up. She's probably married by now."

"Or she's been pining away the years, waiting for her man to come home from the sea," she said.

"Let's not talk about it," I said. "Enjoy the day."

"It's beautiful here," she said.

"Too bad there's nothing for many miles," I said. "Can't stay here without food and water."

"That's part of what makes it special," she said. "No people."

"Just you and me," I said.

We spent the rest of the day playing in the water and napping on the beach. We had a late lunch on Holly's boat, before preparing to leave. The weather was holding, but we had no way to get a forecast in this remote spot. There was no point in hanging around until it got worse. It was time to go.

We poked our noses out past the southern tip of Big Sand Cay. The sea was almost calm. We steered clear of Three Mary's rocks, and dialed in our courses for Luperon. Holly was motor sailing. There wasn't enough wind to move her very fast. I was humming along at seven knots, checking gauges and listening to the familiar sounds of the engine. Over the thousands of hours I'd sat behind the wheel, I was tuned in with my vessel. The engine made a certain sound when all was well. I could hear when she was happy. I knew what the gauges should read at all times. I knew how she handled different types of seas. I listened to the waves that were parted by her hull. When it was calm, and everything was perfect, there was a harmony to the combination of sounds and vibrations.

I watched Holly add sail and make adjustments. She changed course to put more wind in her sails. She fiddled and tuned. She was feeling the vibe of her vessel just like I had done. We were two little specks in a great blue sea, always searching. I wanted to find peace and love. Holly wanted to find adventure. This would be our last trip together.

The winds picked up around midnight. I hated wind at night. I couldn't see the waves like I could in the daytime. By two in the morning, the winds had built to twenty knots and the waves were getting angry. By four we experienced a full-blown gale. We couldn't turn back and there was no place to hide. I was forced to fall off course and aim for one of those bays to the west of Luperon. Holly was down to just her main, and it was fully reefed. I hope she remembered what I'd told her about not fighting the wind. I tried to call her on the radio, but she didn't answer. I lost her in the waves. It was too dark to see her. Clouds blocked the moon.

I hung on through the night, trying to hold course and trying to see Holly. I was only two hours from landfall when I heard a change in the sounds. The engine put off a higher pitch. The boat slowed slightly. RPM's were up, but the speed was down. The temperature was up. Oil pressure was okay. The battering of the waves eased up. Something remained amiss with the engine. I grabbed a flashlight and checked the exhaust. There was no smoke. Water poured out normally. I opened the main hatch to the engine room. There was steam coming off the transmission. It was very hot. The engine was running freely and seemed fine. The transmission was out of synch or slipping.

I went back to the wheel and took it out of

gear. I coasted for a minute. When I put it back in forward, it made a grinding sound. The transmission was failing. I made it into the lee of the big island of Hispaniola. The waters calmed. *Miss Leap* limped along at four knots into the bay at La Isabela. Holly wasn't there. She should have beat me there. I couldn't hail her on the radio. I dropped the anchor and shut everything down. I waited for the engine and transmission to cool off. This was a delayed reaction to her near sinking way back in Fort Myers. I thought I'd gotten all the water out by continuously changing the fluid. Now I had a serious problem in a third world country.

I only had a few hours left before the winds would pick back up. If I didn't leave soon, I'd miss the good window to get into Luperon. I didn't want to get caught in rough conditions with a sick vessel. That could be disastrous. I drained the transmission, burning my arm on the still hot casing. I saw metal shavings in the fluid. That wasn't a good sign. I refilled it and drained it again. It took three times before I got no more shavings in the catch pan. I started the engine and put it in gear. There was no grinding noise. I had no choice but to make a run for it.

I pulled up anchor and went back to sea,

working my way up the north coast. The transmission held together for over an hour. Just outside the entrance to Luperon Harbor it slipped badly. I slowed to three knots. Smoke poured out of the engine room hatch. I'd burned it up. I was still limping along though. I hailed the harbor's Commandancia over the radio. He recognized me. He knew me a little too well. I had to assure him that my passport was in order before he would grant entrance. I pleaded with him for help, citing my mechanical difficulty. He sent out a small boat to assist. I threw a line to the men aboard, and they towed me into the harbor. I shut down the engine on the way in.

The men told me to drop my anchor after they positioned me near the government dock. The Customs greeting party was on me in minutes. The smoke coming through the floor boards was enough to hurry them along. They stamped my passport and asked me to see the Commandancia at my earliest convenience. He'd have to wait.

I opened the hatch to see what was going on in the engine room. The stuffing box was leaking at a good rate. Water had pooled around the transmission. It was so hot that it quickly turned the water to steam. I checked to make sure the bilge pump was keeping up with the flow. It was. I grabbed some wrenches and tightened the packing nuts. The flow decreased but it didn't stop. The shaft must have heated up and cooked the packing. I was at anchor in a safe harbor. I wasn't leaving anytime soon. My boat was damaged and not going anywhere. Where the hell was Holly?

I needed to go to shore to talk to the Commandancia. I needed to find someone who could repair or replace my transmission. I didn't want to leave until I knew that Holly was safe. I hailed her on the radio. To my surprise, she answered.

"I'm outside the entrance," she said. "Not sure how to get in. I almost ran aground once already."

"Did you call the harbormaster?" I asked.

"No, not yet," she replied.

"Hail them and ask for a pilot boat," I told her. "Someone will come out and lead you in. I'm up by the main dock. *Miss Leap* is broken."

"What happened?" she asked.

"Come on over when you get settled," I said. "I'll tell you all about it."

"See you soon," she said.

I was glad she was okay. I rechecked the bilge and the pumps had beaten the incoming water. I got the stuffing box down to just a steady drip. I could deal with that, for now. There was always a lot of boats in the harbor here. There had to be a mechanic available. It could have been worse. I could have broken down in some remote outpost with no chance of getting help.

*Another Adventure* came into view. The same little boat that had towed me in was leading her through the tricky entrance channel. I'd have to find those fellows and give them a tip later. Holly got her anchor down and immediately lowered her dinghy. She came over to find out what was going on.

"The transmission is fried," I told her. "I'm stuck here for a bit."

"That sucks," she said. "Anything I can do to help?"

"We'll have to go see the big chief around here," I said. "But you didn't wait for Customs. We'll go in to town after they check you in. What took you so long to get here, by the way?"

"I did just like you told me," she said. "It got pretty snotty so I rode with it. I holed up at Punta Rucia for the night."

"Good girl," I said. "I made it into La Isabella. Now go wait for Customs. I'll pick you up when I see them leave."

The Customs and Immigration officers spent a lot of time on Holly's boat. They probably didn't get to visit with pretty young ladies very often. I went to get her as soon as they left. We reported directly to the Commandancia.

"I have checked your passport with the State Department," he said. "You are legal this time."

"I went through great pains to rectify that situation," I told him. "Just so I could see your smiling face again."

"I doubt it was my ugly face you came to see," he said, looking over at Holly. "But we'll discuss that later, if you wish."

I nodded and we continued with the formalities of checking into the country. I introduced him to Holly.

"A different lovely lady each time through," he said. "Always a delight for the community."

"I'm going to need a trustworthy mechanic," I told him. "Transmission work."

"Find Big Papa down at the old boatyard," he said. "I believe he knows a thing or two about them."

"Thanks," I said. "I'll be around at least until I get fixed up."

"Welcome to Luperon again, Breeze," he said. "Enjoy your time here."

We were on shore, so we decided to stop at one of the dusty little houses that served dinner to gringos. We each got a plate of chicken with rice and beans. Adding two Presidente beers ran our total bill to eight dollars. We discussed our difficult passage.

"I have to admit," she said. "That was a hell of a rough ride."

"It's going to be like that from here all the way to the BVI," I said. "Except you'll be beating straight into it."

"I think I'll wait here while you get repaired," she said. "Look for lighter winds. They have internet here?"

"You're Bahamas phone won't work," I said. "But there's a couple cafes in town with wifi."

"Show me tomorrow," she said. "Let's get some rest before we hunt down a mechanic."

"I'm tired of being tired," I admitted. "I'm glad you are going to sit tight for a while. We'll have a little more time together."

"How are we going to say goodbye?" she asked.

"Feels like we already did back there at Big Sand Cay," I said.

"But here we are," she said.

"We'll figure something out," I said. "Right now I need to worry about my boat. You worry about your weather window."

We retired to our separate boats. I tried to come up with an appropriate gesture for saying goodbye when the time came. It was a difficult mental exercise. Holly wasn't a flowers and candy kind of girl. I gave up. The problem of a failed transmission kept taking priority. I vowed to track down Big Papa first thing in the morning.

Having dismissed my immediate problems for the time being, I turned to rum to drown them properly. I sat on the aft deck, alternating drinks of beer with shots of rum. Holly was not above decks. It was time to start practicing being alone. Once my brain was sufficiently pickled, I put the rum away and hit the sack.

My previous dream repeated itself. I was chasing Holly on the deep blue sea. She got farther and farther away until she disappeared. When she was gone, I turned to go, but to where?

I went back to shore by myself first thing in the morning. I walked the docks of the old boatyard. Big Papa found me. He was a huge black man with gnarled hands. His khaki work shirt was covered in grease. He wore a big straw hat to block the sun. It was marked with greasy fingerprints.

"Can I help you?" he asked.

"You Big Papa?" I asked.

"Depends on who's asking," he said.

"A guy with a blown up transmission," I said. "The Commandancia told me to look you up."

"Is it inline or a drop down?" he asked.

"Runs straight out of the motor," I told him.

He asked what the brand name was, what motor it was attached to, and if I had enough money to pay him. I assured him I had the money, in American dollars.

"If you ain't in a hurry, I can order a new one, or parts to rebuild," he said. "Comes from Virginia."

"Any other options?" I asked.

"I got sort of a boat graveyard," he said. "I could check them old trawlers for something that would work. That setup was pretty common."

"Give it a shot," I said. "If not, we'll just have to order what we need."

"I'll come out this afternoon and take a look," he said. "Might be some parts we could scavenge somewhere."

I thanked him and said I'd be back on board by noon. I walked up the hill and into the center of town. I remembered Andi's clinic from my last visit. It was painted with bright pastels. She'd grown flowers in window boxes on either side of the front door. Small patches of neatly trimmed green grass lined the sidewalk. It was only a few blocks from the waterfront. I hadn't planned to see her, not while Holly was still around. Something drew me down the street towards her clinic. It built momentum and I couldn't turn around.

She wasn't there. The flower boxes were empty. The grass was overgrown and brown. The front door was boarded up. She was gone. My heart sunk. I didn't even know why, but I felt sad that she wasn't there. Did I have the silly notion that I could replace Holly with Andi, just like that? I hadn't really thought about it. The difficult passage and my crippled boat were first and foremost on my mind. I sat down on a bench outside the empty clinic and wondered where she'd gone.

I'd had my chances with her. I'd let her go. Hell, she'd had her chances with me. She'd let me go too. When we were young and in love, the world had conspired to tear us apart. When we reunited as older, wiser adults, the time just wasn't right. I'd always thought of her as the one that got away, until I'd gotten close to Holly. Since Holly and I had joined forces, I hadn't thought about any of the women from my past.

One of the men who'd helped both Holly and I get into the harbor came walking along. I stopped him and offered some cash. I told him to share it with the other men on the boat. He was grateful.

"What happened to her?" I asked, pointing to the empty clinic.

"New building," he said. "Other side of town."

"She's still here?" I asked.

"Si, senor," he answered.

She was here after all. My heart skipped a beat, like it did whenever I had been in her presence. I didn't have time to cross town, though. I had to meet Big Papa. I hurried back down to the docks and hopped in my dinghy. Holly was just pulling up. I felt guilty, even though she couldn't read my thoughts.

"I've got a mechanic coming out to look at my boat," I told her.

"Dinner later?" she asked.

"Sure," I answered. "You want to go into town or cook something?"

"Town, if you're buying," she said.

"No problem," I said. "I'll pick you up later."

I didn't think that Big Papa would fit down in the engine compartment. He managed to lay over the open hatch and turn his wrenches. As things started to come apart, transmission fluid poured into the bilge. It combined with the excess water from the leaky stuffing box and was pumped overboard by the bilge pump. Nobody here cared about polluting the harbor. Most of the boats were flushing their heads overboard too. Cruisers who didn't see the charm in the place called it Pooperon.

"These teeth here got rusted," said Big Papa. "Some of them broke off and gummed up the works."

"Do I need a new one?" I asked. "Or can you get new guts for it?"

"I got a ghost trawler over there with the same motor," he said. "Different transmission but it will bolt right on."

"How do we know if it's any good?" I asked.

"Won't, till we try," he answered. "I'll take it apart and clean it all up first."

"I appreciate it," I said. "You need any money up front?"

"You ain't going nowhere with no transmission," he said. "Give me few days. I'll bring it out here after I go over it real good."

He took his little work boat back towards the boatyard. It wasn't much of a boatyard anymore. It was a collection of dilapidated docks and half-sunk fishing boats. He was scratching out a living off the cruisers and full-time liveaboards in the harbor. I had no idea what he would charge me. There was no estimate given, no paperwork.

# Eighteen

I cleaned up the grease from where Big Papa had been laying. I was on my hands and knees when I heard an outboard motor approaching. There was a knock on the hull. It was Holly.

"Any progress," she asked.

"A very large, grease-covered black man is bringing me a used transmission out of an old trawler," I told her. "Won't know if it works until we put it in and try it. It'll be a few days."

"It's still blowing like stink out there," she said. "I won't have a window for at least a few days."

Luperon Harbor was so protected that you couldn't tell if the wind was blowing or not. The mountains rose up all around us. Other than the filthy water, it was a great place to be holed up in foul weather. I was stuck, and Holly was sticking around.

"You want to go for dinner again?" I asked. "Your turn to buy."

"Hop in," she said. "I'll drive too."

She took me to Pescaderia Liche. The special was fried fish. There was no mention of what species it was, but it was good. It was served over rice with plantains instead of beans. We were just finishing up when I heard a familiar voice behind me.

"Of all of the gin joints in all the towns in the world, you walk into mine," the voice said.

It was Andi. I turned to look at her. She was as stunning as ever. My heart fluttered like she always caused it to do. Other than a few fine streaks of silver in her dark hair, she hadn't aged. Her smile was seductive. Her brown eyes sparkled with silver flecks.

I stood and went to her. We hugged politely and held each other at arm's length.

"You look just like a twenty year old college girl I once knew," I said.

"You look great, Breeze," she said. "Your lady friend must have you eating healthy."

"Holly, this is Andi," I said. "Andi, this is Holly."

"Pleased to meet you," said Holly.

"Likewise," said Andi. "The last time Breeze was here, he had a darling Cuban girl aboard. Whatever happened to her?"

"I took her to some family in Baltimore," I said.

"And then you rode off into the sunset," she said.

"Something like that," I said.

"He'll break your heart too someday," she said to Holly. "It's what he does."

"We have an understanding," said Holly. "We're just enjoying the ride."

"Good for you," Andi said.

Andi looked at me with an interesting smile. She curled a strand of hair around one finger.

"I thought maybe you'd settled down with one of these pretty young girls you always seem to find," she said. "It's been a long time. What brings you to our little town his time?"

"Holly is a sailor," I began. "She's off to see the world. My boat is temporarily out of commission. We were both lucky to make safe harbor here."

I could sense Andi digesting that information. I'd telegraphed that Holly was leaving, without me.

"Don't let me interfere with your remaining time together," she said. "Nice to see you again, Breeze. Nice to meet you, Holly."

She walked to the door and stopped. She turned around to look back at us. She gave a little wave and a big smile, and left.

"I thought Taylor was pretty," said Holly. "Andi is like a supermodel."

"I can't disagree," I said.

"How do you do it?" she asked. "I mean you're good looking, but all these ex-girlfriends are gorgeous. They seem out of your league. What are you doing with me?"

"I won't answer that last question except to say that you're as pretty as they are, just different," I said. "As to how I do it, how did I get to you?"

"You just sort of grew on me, I guess," she said. "You have a very good way about you when we're one on one. There's just something about you."

"Pretty girls in a bar don't give me a second look," I said. "My charm only works once I get to know someone."

"You must have really had it working to get in her pants," she said. "I can't believe how beautiful she is. She took my breath away."

"She does it to me, too," I admitted. "I'd almost forgotten what it was like to be around her."

"What happened with you two?" she asked. "Did you leave her to ride off into the sunset? You need your head examined."

"She left me because I was in no way ready," I said. "Then I left her to help a pretty young Cuban girl start a new life in America."

"Let me guess," she said. "The Cuban girl was a knockout too."

"Nothing happened between us," I said. "I just had a mission to help her."

"Breeze and his famous missions," she said. "I've got an idea for you, Breeze. You're stuck here with a broken boat. You have no mission. You've got no particular place to be. I'm leaving soon. You should go to that beautiful woman and do whatever it is you need to do to get her back."

"With your blessing?" I said.

"At my urging," she said. "It will make it easier for me to say goodbye."

"I'm not looking forward to saying goodbye," I said.

"Me neither," she said.

"Let's go back and get hammered," I offered. "I've got plenty of rum left."

"Excellent idea," she said.

Holly drank with me shot for shot. We pulled out the charts and I gave her my best advice on her upcoming travels. I used my finger to map her through the Mona Passage. I showed her all the likely anchorages on the south coast of Puerto Rico. I explained that she didn't need to go through Customs and Immigration in Puerto Rico or the USVI. I told her she'd have to go to Tortola to check into the BVI. I showed her my favorite spots on Jost Van Dyke and Norman Island. I suggested a side trip to Anegada, even though I'd never been there.

"You're on your own after that, sweetheart," I said. "That's as far as I've been."

She used her own finger and stabbed assorted islands on the chart.

"Martinique, Anguilla, Nevis," she said. "Aruba, Bonaire, Guatemala."

"To Holly and *Another Adventure*," I said, raising my shot glass.

"Here's to tall ships. Here's to small ships. Here's to all the ships at sea," she said. "But the best ships are friendships. Here's to you and me."

"May your departures equal your landfalls," I said.

She laughed and put her head on my shoulder. We were good and rightly drunk. I took her glass and set it down. She laid her head on my lap.

"You're gonna miss me when I'm gone," she said.

"No doubt about that," I said. "You're the best friend I ever had."

"Best friend," she said, before passing out.

I just sat there with her sleeping on my lap. The one dread with the red ribbon was covering one eye. I moved it aside. I watched her breasts rise and fall with her breathing. I went back to our days walking the beaches of the Berry Islands. I pictured her pure joy when we got her boat back from the shop. I pictured her standing at the helm of her boat, flying her bikini top like a flag in the wind. We'd packed a million memories into a few months of time. Now, our time was about to come to an end. I laid my head back and joined her in sleep.

When I woke up in the morning, I was laying down with no head in my lap. Holly was gone. She'd stuck a note on the coffee maker.

*Go see your new girlfriend. I could see it in her eyes, Breeze. She still loves you.*

# Nineteen

I swung through the old boatyard and found Big Papa sweating over a rusty transmission.

"Bolts is all froze up," he said. "Gonna be another day, at least."

I walked up the hill and into town. I was taking Holly's advice. I was going to see Andi. I found her new building on the outskirts of town. To the right of the front door was a bronze plaque. It read; Andrea Mae Mongeon Clinic for Care. I took a deep breath went inside.

"Nice digs," I said.

"The government actually came through with a grant," she said. "Isn't it great?"

"I'm proud of you," I said. "This is real nice. You're doing good things here."

"It's a nice life," she said.

"But it still doesn't involve a man?" I asked.

"All you have to do is stay," she said.

She could have hit me with a stick. I stood there dumbfounded. She did that hair twirling thing again. I saw her as a twenty year old girl, sexy and intriguing.

"You'd still have me?" I asked. "After all that's happened between us?"

"You've always been the one," she said. "But you've been a hard man to love. You don't know how it made me feel to see you back here, and to see you with another woman, again."

"Holly and I had come to terms with splitting up before we got here," I said. "I think my inner self secretly hoped to find you still here. I didn't want to admit it to myself."

"Do you love her?" she asked.

"I will miss her terribly," I answered.

"Dancing around the question," she said. "I'll let you off the hook on that one. Now, did you love me?"

"I loved you when we first met," I said. "When you came back into my life after all those years, I wanted to love you again. I wanted it so bad."

"But your wife had just died and you were all fucked up in the head," she said.

"I hope you realize how grateful I am for the way you helped me," I said.

"I was the right person at the right time," she said. "God works in mysterious ways."

"I usually say that shit works out," I said.

"But it didn't work out for us back then," she said. "And now it's not working out for you and Holly."

"It's not her fault," I said. "And it wasn't your fault either."

"What's she like?" asked Andi.

"You saw her," I said. "She's a funky, hippie, sailor girl. She is what she looks like. No pretense whatsoever."

"Sounds a lot like you," she said. "You're a funky, boat bum, sailor guy with no pretense."

"We were friends first," I said. "Then we became cautious lovers. We both knew what we were looking for. We got real close, to be honest, Andi. We almost found it with each other."

"Congratulations," she said. "You were screwing the female Breeze. She's you, with tits."

"No wonder I liked her so much," I said.

"Freud would probably have a field day with it," she laughed.

"Probably why we can't stay together," I said. "She's too much like me."

"Except twenty years younger," she said. "When was the last time you were with a woman your own age?"

"It was you," I said.

"Let me assure you," she said. "I'm every bit as good as those younger women, but with more experience."

"You were a fantastic lover," I said.

"Was it fantastic with Holly?" she asked.

"Once when we were under sail," I said. "That was pretty close. Then the day we realized we were splitting up, after we decided, it was the most real and honest thing. I won't soon forget it."

"The two of you finally loved each other, after you called it quits," she said. "My one year of philosophy fails me."

"The pressure was gone," I said. "We were really very close. It just didn't come together until we gave up on finding it."

"She must be a special person," she said.

"I'm lucky to have known her," I said. "But I'll be happy for her. I hope she finds adventure."

"What about you?" she asked. "What will you do now?"

"I don't know," I said. "I need to digest things. Holly is leaving soon. I haven't figured out how to say goodbye. Now I'm sitting here with you, remembering why I loved you so long ago. It's a lot for a simple man to ponder."

"If you were a simple man, the decision would be easy," she said. "You'd stay here with me and live happily ever after. Give me half a chance. You'll forget that girl, and whoever else you've been diddling."

"It's so good to see you again, Andi," I said. "Great to talk with you. Being here like this just thrills me inside. You've always been able to do that to me, but give me time."

"Go do your thing," she said. "My offer comes from deep within my heart, but if you go, I'll understand. Just don't run off without saying goodbye."

"I'll see you soon," I said. "And thanks."

I stopped at the little market and picked up some groceries. Holly and I had gone through a good portion of our stores. We hadn't been to an island with a grocery store for a long time. I also grabbed a couple bottles of rum. It was cheap there. I loaded my goodies on the boat and saw Holly coming out in her dinghy. She was hauling jerry jugs for more water. A little while later she came by again with her own groceries. On the third trip, she stopped at my boat.

"How do we get fuel here?" she asked.

"There's a guy up at the docks that will bring it out in drums and pump it into your boat," I said. "Best to filter it. He won't mind."

"Great thanks," she said. "Looks like the weather will be right in a few more days."

"I've been thinking about," I said. "When I get a transmission, I'll need to give it a test run. Maybe I'll run as far as Samana with you."

"You're not hooking up with Andi?" she asked.

"She's offered," I said. "I haven't made up my mind. Too sudden."

"You're a damn fool," she said. "But you're welcome to tag along."

"I can turn around and go back," I said. It will be a good test. Stop by when you finish running errands, I'll fix dinner."

"I've got a ton of shit to do," she said. "I want to plot courses on the GPS like you showed me. I have to store all this food. I'll catch up with you tomorrow."

"Suit yourself," I said.

She went about her business. I sat on my trawler alone. I was low on fuel too. I decided to wait until he came out to fuel Holly. I couldn't do shit until Big Papa was finished. I started to get a beer, but stopped. I was suddenly very tired, mentally and physically. The combination of injuries that I'd incurred, the constant traveling, keeping up with the much younger Holly, all had combined to wear me down. Holly was leaving. Andi wanted me to stay. What did I want? For the first time in a long time, I was at a loss. I didn't know what to do next. I'd had plenty of downtime over the years, but it was spent in the familiar confines of Pelican Bay. That lovely little bay off Cayo Costa was home.

I was temporarily stuck thousands of miles away from home. A very special person was about to disappear from my life, most likely forever. It was depressing. On the other hand, a very desirable woman lived there. I knew her intimately. She wanted me to stay with her.

The implied choice Holly had given me was to give up *Leap of Faith* and go off with her to see the world, or to let her go on her own. The choice Andi had given me was to stay in the Dominican with her. What would become of my boat then? She'd probably rot in the stinking harbor of Luperon, while I was off loving another woman. My head started to hurt. My mind bounced around from Holly to Andi to *Miss Leap*.

The only solid conclusion I was able to reach, was that I owed my allegiance to *Leap of Faith*. I could never leave her. I couldn't go with Holly on *Another Adventure*. Chasing her in my boat was killing *Miss Leap*. If I stayed with Andi, my boat would most certainly be neglected. I could come out and check on her. I could try to keep up with her maintenance, but it wouldn't be the same as living aboard full-time. Was there a compromise? I could consider it, but would Andi?

I gave up thinking and went for that beer. One turned into six. Catching a buzz in the afternoon sun made me sleepy. I laid down. I was so tired. I cringed at the thought of getting old. I wanted to blame it on the damage my body had suffered and the constant travel. I just needed some rest.

I ended up sleeping through dinner and all through the night. It was a dark and dreamless sleep. My body never moved. I woke up fully clothed, in the same position that I'd first laid. It took me a minute to figure out where I was. I turned on the coffee maker and stuck my head outside. I was still stuck in Pooperon. I sat down and sipped coffee, trying to clear the cobwebs from my mind. I needed a transmission. I needed fuel. I needed breakfast. I needed to figure out what I was going to do with my life.

I saw the work boat with fifty-five gallons drums come out into the harbor. I waved him down.

"I fill the rasta girl first," he said. "I'll come back for you."

He went over to Holly's boat. She'd take less than one drum to be full. I'd take all the rest. Soon after the fuel delivery was finished, Big Papa came out with my transmission. He'd cleaned it up and painted it red to match my engine. It looked almost brand new. I helped him haul it aboard and ease it down into the engine compartment. It bolted in place nicely. He made all the necessary connections. I filled it with fluid. We started the engine and shifted in and out of gear. It sounded fine. The shaft turned. It didn't appear to be warped. Too much water dripped out of the stuffing box when the shaft turned. Big Papa changed it out with the boat still in the water. It made me nervous, but he obviously knew what he was doing. The extra water that drained into the bilge was pumped out by the pumps, taking excess fluids with it. It left a purple sheen on the water around my boat.

He offered to send someone out to clean the waterline and scrape the barnacles off my boat's bottom and running gear. I accepted. There was no way I was getting in that water. Eventually, nothing else needed to be done. It surprised me. I could leave any time I wanted, if that's what I chose to do. Holly hailed me on the radio.

"I'm leaving in the morning," she said. "You get squared away?"

"Everything is good to go," I said.

"You still want to come with me to Samana?" she asked.

"I'll let you know."

Holly had made herself scarce since our drunk fest. I knew she was busy, but it was clear she was avoiding me. She either was trying to clear the way for Andi, or she just didn't want to say goodbye. She was putting some distance between us even before she pulled up anchor. For the moment, that left me to deal with the question of Andi. There was one last option that we hadn't considered. I went to lay out my proposal to her.

I walked into her place and she gave me a huge smile.

"God, look at you," she said.

"What?" I asked. "Do I have ketchup on my shirt or something?"

"No silly," she said. "You're just so utterly different than other men. You've got that rugged, tanned, seafarer look going on. Makes my heart go pitter patter."

"We're even then," I said. "I still get butterflies around you."

"We should do something about that," she said.

"Maybe we will," I said. "Remains to be seen. Let me ask you something. Are you happy and fulfilled here?"

"Very much so," she said. "I live a simple life of service. The people are wonderful. I avoid all politics unless it involves this little village. The people take care of me. I take care of them. So yes, I am happy. The unanswered question in my life has always been you, Breeze."

"You haven't been sitting here waiting for me to show up, I hope."

"I've always left room for that possibility," she said. "Now here you are."

"I had a discussion with some wonderful friends about the meaning of life," I told her. "What we want out of it. Holly wants to sail. Fred wants to enjoy his retirement on his yacht in Georgetown."

"I remember Captain Fred," she said. "Very interesting man. But what about you, Breeze? What do you ultimately want out of life? It seemed like you were searching for it with Holly, but you're letting her go."

"That one special woman and me, alone in an island paradise," I said. "Free from the cares of life. Nothing to do but share our hearts, souls, and bodies."

"Sounds wonderful," she said.

"Come with me, Andi," I said. "I'll feed you fresh fish and lobster. I'll walk with you on sandy beaches. I'll make love to you under the stars. I will finally, completely, give myself to you."

She was silent for several minutes. She walked around her office, looking at pictures. She picked up small mementos and put them back down. She stood with her back to me. She didn't speak for a full minute. When she turned to face me, she had little tears trying to escape from the corner of her eyes.

"You make my heart ache, Breeze," she said. "Please stay here with me. Love me here in this world. Don't leave me again."

"All I do lately is make pretty girls cry," I said.

"I wish you could understand what you do to women," she said.

Now it was my turn to be left speechless. The decision was upon us. I could stay with her. She could come with me, or never again would we meet. Our answers would be final. Each would shape the path of the other's future.

"Please stay," she said.

"I can't," I said. "Please come with me."

"I can't, she said.

Her tears made me want to cry. I wanted to turn and run from her office as fast as I could. I felt like a complete jackass. My only real skill was breaking women's hearts. I went to her and held her close.

"I'm sorry I can't come with you," she said. "It's my fault. I won't make your dream come true."

"Nonsense," I said. "It's clearly my fault. Any man in his right mind would stay here with you."

"I hope you find her someday," she said. "I wish you love and happiness."

"Love and happiness," I said. "Andi, you're a fine girl. What a good wife you would be."

"But your life, your love and your lady, is the sea," she said. "I always loved that song."

"I need to go," I said. "Before I change my mind."

"Where will you go?" she asked.

"I'm tired," I said. "I just want to go home."

"Godspeed."

# Twenty

I went by Holly's boat to tell her that I would follow her in the morning. She shook her head at me and asked me to come aboard. She was going over charts for the north coast of the Dominican Republic.

"Weather still good?" I asked.

"Winds are supposed to be light out of the southeast," she said. "It will be flat along the coast."

She drew a line with her finger on the chart.

"I'm going to angle out to the north until I get some wind," she said. "Stay inside of me and you should have smooth water. Try to keep up."

"If there's good wind out there you'll be way faster," I said. "Just go in ahead of me and anchor. I'll find you when I get there."

"I still haven't figured out how to say goodbye," she said. "Makes me sick thinking about it."

"Relax," I said. "We'll worry about it in Samana. Keep your mind on the journey. Stay sharp."

"I wrote you a letter," she said. "Just in case, but you can't read it until I'm gone."

I put the envelope in my pocket and kissed her on the forehead.

"It's a great big world out there," I said. "Enjoy every bit of it."

"I want to leave as soon as they pull those nets in the morning," she said. "See you in Samana."

"See you in Samana," I said.

I went back to my boat. I'd been ending up there alone almost every night. I didn't mind. Being alone with my boat was the natural order of things. It was only when other people came around that things got screwed up. I started thinking about Pelican Bay. I pictured cruising up the west coast of Florida again. I longed for my home waters. I latched onto the idea of home. There was no reason that my mind had to be made up. I could go ashore and be with Andi at any moment. I could hitch a ride with Holly, or continue to follow her, but home was calling.

Home would soothe my soul. Home would heal my wounds. Home would take me in and make me whole. It was a long way off, but I didn't need to hurry. As long as I was headed in the right direction, I'd be okay. In the meantime, beer and rum would keep me company.

I cracked a cold one and watched Holly take the covers off her sails. She was itching to go. I felt oddly liberated. I didn't have to chase her anymore. I didn't have to live her dream, or conform to what she wanted me to be. I didn't have to live ashore in order to have a life with Andi. I didn't have to live my life for anyone else. I was my own man. That was my best, and worst quality. I was at peace with it. It was the life I'd chosen.

Dawn came early. Holly had her motor running

before my coffee was ready. I fired up my engine and shifted in and out of gear a couple times. The transmission was working fine. The gauges settled in their normal range. All systems were go.

Holly waved and starting pulling up her anchor. I waved back and pulled up mine. The last few yards were covered in muck and slime, making a mess out of the foredeck. I looked up from the windlass and saw Andi standing on the dock. I waved a muddy hand. She waved and turned away. I watched her walk up the hill and back into town.

I drifted for a minute so I could wash the mud off my hands. *Another Adventure* was heading out. I climbed to the bridge and motored after her. As soon as we cleared the harbor, Holly's sails went up. There was very little wind at first. She steered to the northeast, away from the coast. About three miles out, her sails caught the wind. She was an eagle, lunging to take flight. Under full sail, she soared across the blue water. Instead of staying inside where the water was calmer, I followed her out to sea.

She was making adjustments and trimming her sails. Her speed increased dramatically. I couldn't keep up. I didn't even try. I just watched her pull away. She put more and more distance between us. Her sails grew smaller on the horizon. I watched until I couldn't see them. She disappeared in the distance, just like in my dreams.

I veered off and headed north, towards Big Sand Cay. I wasn't going to Samana. I couldn't say goodbye to Holly. She was gone.

I took my boat out of gear and drifted. I pulled the letter out of my pocket.

> *Dearest Breeze,*
>
> *I'm really bad at goodbyes, but this one is the worst. I want you to know that you've given me life. You did your best to give me love. I've learned so much from you. I've learned about this life, and living it to the fullest. I've learned to be true to myself. I can never repay you for those lessons. I tried to love you too. Now, we part. If you're ever in some exotic port, look for Another Adventure in the harbor. You'll always have a friend.*
>
> *I'm not stopping in Samana. Sorry, but I can't bear to say goodbye. I'm taking the Mona Passage all the way to Boqueron and beyond. I'm going to run with the wind and never stop. I owe it all to you. I'll never forget you, Breeze.*
>
> *Always,*
> *Holly*

We pulled the same move on each other, sailing away to avoid the goodbye. Fair enough. She really was a lot like me.

*Godspeed, Holly. I'll never forget you.*

I looked back towards the entrance to Luperon. There was still time. I could make it back before dark if I wanted to.

*Godspeed Andi. I'll never forget you, either.*

I put the transmission in gear and headed north, away from Luperon.

*We're going home, Miss Leap.*

If you enjoyed this book, please leave a review at Amazon.

# Author Notes

I hope you enjoy reading this series as much as I enjoy writing it. Breeze and I have become close friends. I will, however, be taking a short hiatus from writing. At the end of March, 2016, I'll be taking my trawler, *Leap of Faith*, to the Bahamas. My lovely wife and I plan to explore the Berry Islands.

We want to walk the white sands of deserted beaches, far from society. We'll eat fresh fish, watch gorgeous sunsets, and make love under the stars.

See you when we get back, if we come back.

Ed and Kim Robinson

kimeandedrobinson@gmail.com

# Acknowledgements

Cover design by http://ebooklaunch.com/

Interior formatting by http://ebooklaunch.com/

Proofreading by Dave Calhoun

# Other Books in this Series

**Trawler Trash**

www.amazon.com/Trawler-Trash-Confessions-Boat-Bum-ebook/dp/B00MWUAROA

**Following Breeze**

www.amazon.com/Following-Breeze-Trawler-Trash-Book-ebook/dp/B00U57DYTW/

**Free Breeze**

www.amazon.com/Free-Breeze-Trawler-Trash-Book-ebook/dp/B013L2EX88/

**Redeeming Breeze**

www.amazon.com/Redeeming-Breeze-Trawler-Trash-Book-ebook/dp/B01BQSF37O/

# Other Books by Ed Robinson

**Leap of Faith; Quit Your Job and Live on a Boat**
www.amazon.com/Leap-Faith-Quit-Your-Live-ebook/dp/B00F3PE5W6/

**Poop, Booze, and Bikinis**
www.amazon.com/Poop-Booze-Bikinis-Ed-Robinson-ebook/dp/B00IA7JLFA/

**The Untold Story of Kim**
www.amazon.com/The-Untold-Story-Kim-Robinson-ebook/dp/B00J44GFKM/

**Find us on Facebook:**
www.facebook.com/quityourjobandliveonaboat/

**Follow Ed's blog:**
https://quityourjobandliveonaboat.com/

**Contact Ed:** kimandedrobinson@gmail.com

Made in the USA
Monee, IL
22 September 2020